"I doubt that we'll be working together."

Max's voice held a sudden sting. "You haven't proved too reliable in the past."

Leah stared at him, searching his face. "I have every intention of producing this play—"

"You had every intention of remaining an actress, too. Why did you give it up?"

"There were reasons," she said stubbornly.

"Which I, obviously, was never privileged enough to know." He smiled with a pleasant malice. "I haven't forgotten how you walked out on me, Leah. I don't think you'll stick to this very long, either."

"That's where you're *wrong!*" She caught her breath. "This play means more to me than you could ever know. And nobody's going to stop me from producing it. Not even you. Especially not you!"

Books by Jacqueline Gilbert

HARLEQUIN ROMANCES

2102—EVERY WISE MAN
2214—COUNTRY COUSIN
2308—SCORPIO SUMMER
2492—THE TRODDEN PATHS
2631—THE CHEQUERED SILENCE

HARLEQUIN PRESENTS

160—DEAR VILLAIN
600—A HOUSE CALLED BELLEVIGNE

These books may be available at your local bookseller.

For a free catalog listing all titles currently available, send your name and address to:

Harlequin Reader Service
P.O. Box 52040, Phoenix, AZ 85072-2040
Canadian address: P.O. Box 2800, Postal Station A,
5170 Yonge St., Willowdale, Ont. M2N 5T5

The Chequered Silence

Jacqueline Gilbert

Harlequin Books

TORONTO • NEW YORK • LONDON
AMSTERDAM • PARIS • SYDNEY • HAMBURG
STOCKHOLM • ATHENS • TOKYO • MILAN

Original hardcover edition published in 1984
by Mills & Boon Limited

ISBN 0-373-02631-5

Harlequin Romance first edition July 1984

For
NEVILLE
actor, director and friend

———————◆◆———————

CHAPTER ONE

As evening drew in, lights began to appear on the New Jersey skyline, and the George Washington Bridge to the north was reflected in the dark, murky depths of the Hudson River. Leah Durrance stood by the window, contemplating the panorama before her, an invited guest to the party, yet not quite part of it, absently listening to the diversity of American voices floating across the room.

'Here's your drink, Leah,' said an English voice behind her, and she swung round and smiled her thanks to her host, taking the proffered glass. 'And what, may I ask, are your first impressions of the Big Apple?' enquired Henry Ross, and she replied instantly:

'Fascinating, noisy and very, very big.'

Henry claimed approvingly: 'Couldn't say better myself. It's all of those, and more, as you'd find out if you were able to stay for any length of time.'

'Why is it called the Big Apple?'

Henry, now joined by his wife, said: 'Celia, two ignorant Brits want you to tell us how New York City became the Big Apple,' and Celia, tucking her arm through that of her husband's, lifted her fine grey eyes from close scrutiny of the watch at her wrist, smoothed away the slightly worried furrows from her brow, and answered, with a smile:

'It's supposed to have originated in the nineteen-twenties by jazz musicians who described New York as being the ultimate, the big time, and working there was having a slice of the apple.' She gave a laugh and shrugged. 'Who really knows? The Big Apple caught on and was later taken up as a promotions symbol for tourism.'

'Most visitors,' Leah said thoughtfully, 'when they refer to New York really mean Manhattan.'

'That's true,' agreed Celia, 'because the tourist attractions are mostly in Manhattan—Broadway theatres, the big shops on Fifth Avenue and Madison, the skyscraper views. It's the centre of business too, but New York actually comprises five boroughs—Manhattan, Staten Island, Brooklyn, Queens and the Bronx.'

'Tell Leah how the Bronx got its name,' urged Henry, and Celia, seeing genuine interest in her guest's face, went on:

'New York, as you know, was originally a Dutch settlement called New Amsterdam . . .'

'. . . until it was invaded by the British,' interrupted Henry glibly, 'in the person of the Duke of York, who called the city after himself.'

'Who's telling this story?' demanded Celia mildly, and Henry made a great show of clamping his mouth together. 'The land on the other side of the Harlem River, the northern boundary of Manhattan Island, belonged to a Dutch burgher named Jonas Bronck and he built a large farmhouse for his family and farmed the land. They were a sociable lot and began to invite New Amsterdam families out to the farm for visits and people would say they were going up to see the Broncks. The spelling got changed along the way.'

'And the Bowery was derived from the Dutch word *bouwerie*, meaning farm,' explained Henry. 'It's a fascinating subject, once you start to delve. Celia's quite an authority.'

'I have to be,' teased his wife. 'I'm an expert on conducted tours, as Henry always has a relative or a business colleague who's longing to see the World Trade Centre or the Empire State.' She smiled at Leah, adding: 'It is a pity you can't stay over. I'd love to take you round.'

'I'm lucky to be here at all,' asserted Leah, turning merry eyes towards Henry. 'Can you imagine Michael's reaction when he was told he had the measles?'

Henry grinned. 'I can. I must say you're a much prettier representative of Walsh Productions than its boss, and it's been a pleasure to do business with you.'

Leah inclined her head, accepting the compliment demurely, remembering the telephone call from Michael, disgruntled and peevish, asking if her passport was up to date; the hurried packing, the quick meeting for instructions and the scramble to Heathrow. Henry Ross will look after you, Michael had said, and although Leah had known Henry and Celia Ross barely three days, she had warmed to their friendly hospitality.

An unlikely alliance, at first glance. Henry was an unprepossessing man, slight of build with receding wispy hair and pale blue eyes behind thick, dark-rimmed glasses. Traces of his cockney ancestors could be heard, now and again, in his voice, and his manner was slightly aggressive. A man who knew where he was going and what he wanted. He had wanted Celia, who came from an old and respected New England family, and it caused quite a family furore when she married the unknown and totally unsuitable Henry Ross. Unlikely alliance or not, the marriage had lasted ten years and the New England family had resigned itself . . . after all, the man did appear to be making money, a panacea for all the ruffled feathers. How he made it—as a theatrical entrepreneur!—was skated over. Celia was a willowy blonde, a cool beauty that, at first, was faintly off-putting, but which hid a shy, warm personality. Leah now said to her:

'One of these days, if I come again, I'll stay longer and take you up on that promise,' and Celia replied:

'I look forward to that.' She looked at her watch again and gave a small sigh. 'We're waiting for that brother of mine. Where can he have got to? Perhaps we should have another pre-dinner drink, Henry?' and she passed an assessing glance over the other guests, dotted around the room. Henry left them, bottle in hand, and Leah, aiming to distract her hostess, murmured:

'You have a beautiful apartment.'

Celia turned to her, pleased. 'Yes, it is, isn't it? Sometimes I have a fleeting hankering for a modern one, but not often. These old buildings are always peeling plaster and crumbling, but that's the price you have to pay for old world charm and space,' and she indicated the high ceiling with its ornate cornice and centrepiece and the beautiful fireplace. 'I know I'd never be really happy anywhere else in New York. We're true West Siders.'

'West Siders?' questioned Leah, and Celia explained:

'That's the term for living west of Central Park, with Fifth Avenue the dividing line. At one time the West Side was *the* place to live, and the East Side only famous for its slums. The slums were eventually torn down and new, modern apartment blocks built, and there's been a reversal. It's smarter to live on the East Side.' She shrugged. 'You go for what suits you best.' She smiled sympathetically. 'I expect it's a bit bewildering.'

Leah returned the smile. 'Yes,' she agreed, 'but it's also exciting and invigorating. The minute I landed at Kennedy I knew I was going to be hooked on New York. That fantastic view of Long Island as the plane comes down, and then driving in, as that amazing skyline grew nearer, I felt as though I'd been here before, it was all so familiar, I'd seen it so often on film. The cabby pointed out various landmarks—I found the Empire State building myself, you can't miss it, can you?—and finding out I was connected with the theatre, he detoured down Broadway and past Times Square, teeming with people and traffic. It was marvellous!'

Celia was amused at Leah's enthusiasm. 'First impressions are interesting, aren't they? You're okay at the Algonquin?'

Leah's brows rose appreciatively. 'My goodness, yes! I'm being terribly spoiled.'

'Good. When I knew you were coming in place of Michael, I wanted you to stay with us,' Celia confessed, 'but Henry said it was better to keep you Midtown, and I guess he's right, it's so much more central to everything—the office, the theatre and the shops.'

'I haven't stepped foot inside a single shop yet,' bemoaned Leah, 'there just hasn't been time.'

'We can't have that. When do you fly home?'

'Tomorrow, mid-afternoon.'

Celia thought for a moment. 'I'll check with Henry, and if you've finished talking business, I'll come for you in the morning. Where do you want to go?'

'That would be wonderful,' enthused Leah. She struggled to think clearly. 'Bloomingdale's ... Macy's ... oh, and Gucci and Balmain. Scribner's book shop. Cartier and Tiffanys.' She stopped for breath and Celia laughed, advising:

'Remember to wear comfortable shoes.' She saw a movement, through the open door, in the hallway, and her expression changed. 'At last! Now we can eat. Excuse me, please, Leah,' and she hurried out of the room.

Leah sipped her drink, waiting quietly, then Henry appeared at her side.

'My recalcitrant brother-in-law has now arrived,' he affirmed, 'so we can go forward to the dining room.' He offered his arm which Leah smilingly took and they followed the other guests into an adjoining room. Heavy darkwood chairs, ornately carved, were placed round an oval table which was set with silverware and crystal glasses upon immaculate white table linen. These were centred by a candelabrum, its dark red candles lit. As Celia was directing guests to their places, Henry said cheerfully:

'You've been introduced to everyone here but Max. Max, your attention, please.' Two guests separated and one turned at the sound of his name. Henry went on: 'Leah, Maxim Calvert, Celia's brother. Max, I'd like you to meet Leah Durrance, from England.'

In a dream Leah stared mesmerised into the face of the man now standing before her. He had been smiling as he had turned, his expression becoming guarded, one of polite inscrutability, the eyes masking, but not quickly enough. Leah was aware of a similar look of shock in their depths, a blazing glitter, quickly hooded. As her hand came up she wondered if he was going to cut her. Anywhere else, perhaps, but at his sister's dinner party he was shackled by good manners. Their hands touched briefly and Max said: 'Miss Durrance,' while Leah managed: 'How do you do?' enunciating like Eliza Doolittle.

They were mercifully parted, Leah to one side of the table with Henry, and Max to the other, with Celia. As she took her seat she shot Max a quick, incredulous glance and found his eyes upon her, piercing and concentrated as a needle of ice, and averted her gaze, outwardly indifferent, inwardly turbulent.

The first course came and went with Leah sitting like a zombie, her head whirling with questions and speculations, and when Henry leaned to refil her wine glass, she forced herself to ask calmly:

'Mr Calvert is your wife's brother?'

'Stepbrother, actually,' Henry replied. 'Max was born in England and his father died when he was about three. His mother married Joss Calvert, who legally adopted him.' He gave her a sharp look. 'I would have supposed Max's name was familiar to you. He seems to divide his working time between England and the States.'

'Yes, indeed,' agreed Leah hastily, omitting to take her knowledge further.

'It was through Max that I met Celia.' Henry grinned. 'The Calverts are high-class New Englanders, very much aware that Celia married beneath her. I take great delight in telling them that I can trace my family tree much further back than they can.'

'You said stepbrother,' prompted Leah, and Henry nodded.

'Joss was a widower with a two-year-old Celia

when he remarried; Max was five.' He leaned closer, eyes twinkling. 'Celia adores Max and is determined to marry him off. Max's intended tonight, the redhead sitting next to him, is from Boston, Massachusetts. Celia has good taste, don't you think?'

Leah murmured her agreement, her eyes dutifully flicking in the redhead's direction. She toyed with her food, although it was delicious, and was grateful to the guest sitting on her other side, a publisher, with whom she talked books. Into one of those odd pauses that can happen on any occasion, he asked why she was in New York. Suddenly the focus of attention, Leah explained:

'I'm here because my boss fell ill,' and Henry clarified:

'Leah works for Michael Walsh and has flown over primarily for one of their British opening nights on Broadway. The play has already had an extended success in the West End of London and should do well here.' He paused and added jokily: 'I hope so, I'm backing it!'

'I understood Miss Durrance to be an actress.' The cool voice with its mid-Atlantic intonation came from across the table.

Leah turned her head and raised her long dark lashes, revealing gold-speckled green eyes as inexpressive as the dark ones that caught and held them, the flickering glow of the candles separating them.

'I used to be,' said Leah. Contact was broken as talk became general. Later, when they had all left the dining room, she was aware that Max Calvert was no longer present. She heard Celia saying to her husband: 'I don't know why. He made a telephone call and then said he had to go. He seemed in a foul mood.'

Leah wondered what her host and hostess would say if she told them that she was the reason for his mood and his absence. The gilt had gone off her visit slightly. More disturbed than she liked to admit, Leah flew back to England and tried to forget him. And succeeded for most of the time.

Snow, which had begun three days earlier, heralding the New Year, was still falling in large white flakes. The Regent Street traffic moved slowly and pedestrians were taking their steps with care, heads down, collars up, against the driving snow.

Leah was undaunted by either the cold or the hazardous conditions and strode along, warmly clad in a honey-coloured fur-collared coat. On her head she wore a matching fur hat, Cossak style, and her legs and feet were snug in thick-knit tights and suede boots. Her dark hair, most of which was hidden beneath the hat, was fringed on the forehead, curving round the face to a little above shoulder-length. Her large, almond-shaped eyes, wide and deeply set, were narrowed against the snowflakes.

As she cut her way through the labyrinth of side streets to her place of work in Shaftesbury Avenue, Leah wondered what the morning had in store for her. She had played a hunch the night before, and only time and Michael Walsh would tell whether it had paid off or not. She entered the building that housed Walsh Productions, taking the lift and walking through the outer office, giving a cheery 'good morning' to the staff as she gained her own office.

This offiice, though small, still gave her an enormous amount of pleasure, especially her own name on the door. She shook the snow from her coat and hat and hung them up, ran a comb quickly through her hair and then sought out Patty Turner in her office.

Patty glanced up at her entrance. 'Good morning, Leah, do you want to see Michael?'

'I think,' began Leah cautiously, 'that he'll be wanting me.'

'Dear me, what have you been doing?' asked Patty, smiling.

'I've found him a play.'

Patty's eyebrows rose. 'Nothing unusual in that, surely?' and Leah grinned, admitting wryly:

'No, but I swopped it for the one he thought he was taking home to read.' Patty tut-tutted and shook her head reprovingly and Leah added: 'What kind of mood is he in?'

Patty pursed her lips. 'He's had a couple of troublesome calls, a few bills in the post, and the twins are cutting teeth.'

'Oh, lord!' groaned Leah, and at that moment the door to the inner sanctum opened and Michael Walsh halted in his stride, holding a manuscript in his outstretched hand. Without preamble, and with deceptive mildness, he asked:

'Do you know who's responsible for this?'

Leah hitched herself from Patty's desk and said: 'Yes, I am.'

If Michael was surprised he did not show it, merely replied:

'Perhaps you'd be good enough to spare me a few minutes?' and glancing at Patty, added: 'Hold all calls, unless urgent, till I tell you otherwise,' before turning and re-entering his office, leaving the door slightly ajar.

Leah raised her brows as she exchanged a speaking look with Patty and followed him in, closing the door behind her. Michael was seated at his desk and he tipped his head towards a chair, motioning Leah to sit. She did so and regarded her boss with a mixture of affection, admiration and gratitude competing with stubborn determination to bring him round to her way of thinking.

Michael was forty-three, of medium height, with an energetic zest for work and play, which showed in his fit, slightly stocky build and his flourishing business. This business had started as a theatrical agency and over the years had extended into production. Michael Walsh had earned the reputation of being an astute man who surrounded himself with bright young men and women, who were encouraged to contribute ideas and take responsibility and initiative.

Leah's own piece of initiative was lying on the desk between them. Mentally crossing her fingers she gave him a bright 'Good morning, Michael' and assumed what she hoped to be a confident and relaxed expression.

Michael nodded his greeting, and after a hard stare, announced portentously: '*The Chequered Silence* by Eliot Yates.' He paused, raised his hands expressively, and declared: 'Never heard of him.'

Leah allowed the merest touch of incredulity into her voice.

'Really, Michael? How odd. You're usually on the ball with all the up-and-coming playwrights.'

'Yes, well, one or two slip through,' acknowledged Michael with heavy sarcasm, fully recognising an opening gambit when he heard one. 'Perhaps you'd fill me in?'

'Certainly.' Leah crossed her legs and rearranged her skirt while she marshalled her facts. 'Eliot Yates is in his thirties, a Cambridge graduate, who has been writing plays since university days ...'

'Who publishes him?' broke in Michael, delivering a loaded question.

'You know he's not been published, Michael, or else you'd have heard of him,' replied Leah with attack, 'and you also know, for you've told us often enough, that new playwrights have to start somewhere. Eliot Yates has been produced. This play happens to be his first on offer to a major production company.'

'I'm honoured,' stated Michael with deep irony. 'Just where have his other epics been staged?'

'They've been professionally performed all over the country by TFTD—Theatre For The Deaf. One of them has recently been televised on a programme covering the Mission for the Deaf.'

'I don't know a great deal about Deaf Theatre.'

'No—and it's a pity. They do wonderful work.'

'Mmm ... *The Chequered Silence* ...' Michael pursed his lips, shooting her a glance from beneath bushy, lowered brows. 'Is Yates deaf?'

Leah shook her head. 'No, but he works with the deaf and partially deaf, as a teacher. That's his job. This is the first play he's written for a majority speaking cast.'

Michael leaned back in his chair, eyeing his assistant throughtfully, saying at last: 'It's too difficult, Leah.'

Disappointment struck Leah quite forcibly, making her voice rise in tone. 'Ah, come on, Michael, since when has that stopped you? You thrive on difficulties!'

'There's a recession on, my dear, surely you've

noticed?' said Michael mildly. 'Our angels, quite rightly, are fearful for their hard-earned money, and a considerable amount is needed to put on a play in the West End these days, as you know full well. Too many businesses collapsing, too many theatres closing down, remaining dark for long periods, and this,' he stabbed the manuscript with a forefinger, 'this is a dicey subject.'

'A neglected one, certainly,' came back Leah passionately. 'Many plays are written around disabilities. Successful ones too. *The Chequered Silence* isn't half as progressive as some. Just the story of a deaf girl who falls in love with her teacher, a hearing man, and he with her.' She rose impatiently to her feet and crossed to the window, staring down on to the busy Shaftesbury Avenue, now whitened by the falling snow. She went on, more calmly: 'I don't know what it is about the deaf. They seem to be a forgotten people—second class citizens.' She turned, her eyes sparkling indignantly. 'Anyone can see when you're blind or crippled, but unless you go around with a large label, who knows if you're deaf? And people haven't much patience with the deaf, because they look so normal. Well! Here's a play to bring attention to a disability that can prove devastating to the sufferers and to those nearest to them. One, moreover, that is set within a compelling story-line, that entertains as well as educates.'

There was a long silence. Michael thumbed through the script. 'Has Yates tried other producers?' he asked presently, and when Leah shook her head, added: 'Why not?'

'I wanted us to have first chance. It's *good*, Michael!'

'And if we do not take it?'

'I'll find someone who will,' Leah replied stubbornly. 'The National, perhaps.'

'I'm flattered I have first option,' Michael acknowledged dryly. 'You know Mr Yates personally?'

'Yes.' Leah saw a speculative gleam enter Michael's eyes and protested quickly: 'But that's not why I'm for it, that's how I got it. Damn it, Michael, it *is* a good play!'

Michael said kindly: 'I wouldn't argue with that. It's well written and has dramatic content, funny too, *but*—and it's a *big* but—it all hangs on the actress who takes the lead. Leah, you've been an actress yourself. There's a hell of an amount of sign language to learn, a mammoth task, like taking on a foreign language.' He closed the manuscript and slapped the palm of his hand downwards. 'The problems are enormous.'

'Not if you're prepared to consider the genuine article,' persisted Leah, leaning persuasively on the desk, '. . . an actress who *is* deaf, who uses sign language every day of her waking life.'

'You know such an actress?'

'I've worked with TFTD and know many, but this particular girl, Nancy Holland, is a wonderful person—bright, intelligent, ideal for the part—and she's extremely experienced, working for TFTD. Really, Michael, it's not the actress you have to worry about, but the actor taking the male lead . . .'

'The speech teacher?'

'Yes. He has to speak all her lines as well as his own, *and* learn sign language—and I mean *learn* it, nothing but the real thing will do. Difficult, but not impossible, given the right actor.'

'I'm sure you've already cast the part in your head,' prompted Michael, and Leah grinned.

'Three or four times over, but my first choice would be Oliver Cape. He's filming at the moment, but we might be lucky with dates. I'll tell you the theatre, too.' She straightened and crossed to a map on the wall showing West End theatres, stabbing a finger at one in particular. 'There's a rumour going round that the King's Theatre will be free in the autumn. If that's true, then it's the right place for a play like *Silence* because it has one enormous advantage.' She paused, and Michael obliged by asking: 'And what's that?'

'The Senheisser system for the hard of hearing. The King's had Senheisser installed last year.' She began to stalk the room. 'All we need is a really good director . . .'

The telephone rang and Michael answered it, saying: 'It's for you. Bristol.'

Leah scowled and took it from him. Michael was not sorry for the interruption. It gave him time to think. He wondered why Leah was sticking her neck out with this particular play. She was emotionally involved, and it intrigued him. He eyed the title page thoughtfully. Was this Eliot Yates the reason? If so, Ruth would be pleased. For the past year his wife had been trying to match Leah with Mr Right and failing.

Michael lifted his eyes, his gaze resting on his assistant. He had to admit that she was a bit of a mystery. He remembered being surprised when Leah had walked into his office, over three years ago, for a job, saying that she had given up acting—or rather, that *it* had given *her* up. This was not unusual, luck played an important part in the profession, but he had always considered her to be an actress with more than her fair share of talent and promise, and she was Nuala Flynn's daughter. That held for something, surely? even if it was only a legacy of green eyes and a low, husky voice.

He had put her on to the agency side, but had quickly transferred her to productions, and it had paid off. Cool, calm, unflappable Miss Durrance had amply fulfilled his early judgment of her capabilities.

Leah caught his eye and mouthed apologies. She was also like her mother in that she lit well on stage, remembered Michael, having good bone structure—striking more than beautiful. It was the eyes, of course, that caught the attention . . . Those eyes were now resting thoughtfully upon him, the telephone call finished, and unabashed, he enquired: 'Ironed out the trouble?' and Leah said darkly;

'Some folk panic about nothing. I shall have to go over, I'm afraid, but it's nothing I can't handle.' She dismissed the call and stood before him, eyeing the script. 'Michael, have you decided anything?'

On an impulse, Michael ignored the question and asked: 'I've never known you so involved before. Tell me why the play's important to you. Is this Eliot Yates someone special?'

She shot him a startled look creasing her brow, and replying absently: 'He's a good friend, and I admire his work for TFTD, but there's more to it than that.' She hesitated and then, as if coming to a decision, walked to the window where she stood for a moment, deep in thought. A snarl-up at one of the road junctions set off a cacophony of horns and she glanced back at Michael. 'Hear that?' she asked. 'The sound of traffic—something we take for granted and grumble about. But not me. Not any more. Now the sound is like music in my ears, because five years ago, Michael, I began to go deaf.'

Michael stared. 'I didn't know that.'

Leah smiled faintly. 'No one knew, except my doctor and my agent. It must have been coming on for some time, but I wasn't aware of anything drastically wrong until I went to my doctor with an ear infection, or so I thought. He sent me for tests and I was eventually told, after a period of time, that I would lose my sense of hearing.'

Michael stirred in his chair, thinking—what a blow for a promising young actress at the beginning of a successful career. He murmured: 'Go on,' and Leah obliged, jauntily derisive.

'I was twenty-three and the world my oyster. Life was sweet and wonderful. I was in love. Offers of work were coming in steadily. Then, suddenly, I was told I had a disease that would make me totally deaf.'

'What happened?' Michael asked gently, and Leah gave a laugh.

'I ran away, that's what happened. Lost my nerve and ran.' She rested her forehead against the cool pane of glass. 'Looking back I'm not particularly proud of the way I behaved, how I reacted, but I've always pulled my full weight in any production, expecting the same in return. How could I begin to ask allowances to be made for me now? It was unthinkable. No half measures, it had to be all or nothing. I was devastated and frightened, the thought of total deafness seemed an awfully lonely existence, so I cut and ran. Backed out of a production of *The Seagull* in which I'd just been cast and went into hiding—not such a difficult task in London.'

'You didn't tell your family?'

Leah shrugged. 'No close family to tell. You know that my mother left her stage career and followed my father all over the world. He was an engineer, and built bridges, and they were killed in a train derailment out in India.'

'I remember,' said Michael. 'Surely you were not on your own?' He hesitated. 'What about this fellow you were in love with?'

Leah turned slowly and said simply: 'I didn't tell him,' and at Michael's expression, added impatiently: 'How could I? He might have felt compelled to stick with me out of pity, and I couldn't have borne that. I was stricken with the panic of being a burden. So I didn't tell him. Even now, I still believe I did right.'

'It might have been fairer if he'd been given the chance to make the choice. However ... and he allowed you to walk out of his life, just like that?'

Leah pulled a face. 'Not really.' She gave a quick sigh. 'Like all relationships, Michael, ours was complicated. His father was ill—stepfather, actually, but he was as close as a real one—and he was up to his neck in work, worried about his father while I was sick with my own secret worries ... tense with waiting for the results of the tests and then desperate when they came through. There was another woman I thought he was interested in, which didn't help, and then he had to leave for the States, because his father had worsened. He was away for ten days. By the time he returned, I'd gone.'

'I see. The poor guy had no say in the matter.'

'It's very easy, looking back, to have doubts,'

Leah went on doggedly, 'but at that point there was no talk of an operation to give me hope for the future.'

'I realise that,' Michael agreed. 'What did you do?'

'I found a job in an office, nothing special. I still had residual hearing, but I didn't know how long I would be able to hold down a job, which made life rather uncertain. Then two things happened.'

'And what were they?'

'After one of my periodic visits to the consultant, I was told he wanted to operate. I consented—for what could I lose?—and was lucky.' She smiled. 'No need to go into how I felt!'

Michael returned the smile. 'No—I can imagine. What was the second thing?'

Her smile broadened. 'You happened. I saw your job advertised. My agent wanted me to go back to acting, but I was reluctant. Two and a half years out had lost me my nerve.' She began to prowl the office. '*You* know what it's like, Michael! "Leah Durrance? Who? Oh, yes, I think I do remember her. What's she been doing? Deaf? Oh, I see . . ." No, thank you, I wasn't going to go through all that. Your job sounded interesting and was connected with the theatre. The rest you know.'

'Don't you miss being a performer?' Michael wafted an impatient hand. 'Do sit down, Leah, you're making me nervous, pacing around like that!'

She grinned and obediently sat. 'Yes and no, but I didn't opt out totally. When I met people at the Deaf Mission where I'd gone with a view to learning sign language, they soon jolted me out of my self-pity, I can tell you! They were wonderful—

happy and uncomplaining, making the best of their lives. I became involved with their theatre and even after my hearing was restored I carried on, because,' and she gave an embarrassed shrug, 'I still feel bound to them.'

Michael said: 'I can understand that.' His eyes narrowed thoughfully. 'What about the fellow you left? Did he ever find out? Did you contact him again?'

Leah gave an incredulous laugh. 'Ah, come off it, Michael! I walked out on him!'

'You never bumped into him, all this time?'

She hesitated. 'Yes, once—last year. He more or less cut me dead.'

The telephone rang again and this time was for Michael. Leah rested chin on hand, switching off Michael's voice, hearing it only as a background murmur. She felt curiously drained. Talking had brought it all vividly back. The despair, the fears, the loneliness—and the memories of Max. She moved restlessly in the chair.

A new, glossy-covered book was lying on the desk by Michael's hand. He shot it across the surface towards Leah, indicating that he was stuck with the call. She picked it up, idly turning the pages. It was a recent publication, profiles of distinguished men and women in the theatrical profession. Each had a full-page photograph and a history. Leah became engrossed, and almost as if it were planned, she turned a page and Max stared up at her.

The photograph was a good one, catching the slightly mocking expression in the dark brown eyes and the faint smile. Looking at it, Leah felt the sudden racing of her pulse, acknowledging resignedly that she still found him wildly attractive.

Not every woman's taste, but the planes and hollows of his face pleased her sense of form and his eyes, compelling, with unusually full upper lids, blazed from the page, taking attention away from the rather beaky nose and long length of jaw.

She dragged her eyes away from the photograph and was half-way through reading the long and impressive list of achievements when Michael replaced the telephone and Leah quickly shut the book, an automatic reaction. She had kept Max hidden for so long it had become second nature to her.

'Sorry about that,' said Michael. 'Good book . . . yes?' he went on, indicating the edition in her hand. She murmured something appropriate and replaced it on the desk. Michael reached for the manuscript and held it out to her. Leah stood, feeling overwhelming disappointment as she took it from him. She managed a smile, saying:

'Thank you for reading it, Michael.'

'That's what I'm here for,' he replied blandly. 'I shall want the usual analysis—figures, names and dates, etc. I'll enquire about the King's Theatre.' He paused, brows raised. 'Well? What are you waiting for?'

Leah stared blankly, and as his words sunk in, her face broke out into incredulous delight.

'Michael! Do you mean you'll do it?' she burst out, and when he nodded, she swept round the desk and gave him an impulsive hug. 'It is a good play, isn't it?' she demanded.

'Yes, it's good,' Michael agreed, 'and you've convinced me it can be done.' He paused. 'And it's all yours.'

This stopped Leah in her tracks. She looked at him, wide-eyed, exclaiming: 'Michael . . .

you mean . . .? My own London production?'

He nodded. 'Now be off with you, or you'll have me forgetting I'm a happily married man!'

Leah chuckled and walked to the door, treading on air. 'You'd run a mile!' she teased, before making an excited exit.

Michael stood for a moment in thought, his eyes absently resting on the glossy theatre profile book. Then, recollecting himself, he slid the volume into the bookcase and settled down to work.

CHAPTER TWO

THE taxi pulled up outside the Savoy Hotel, and after paying the man at the wheel, Leah hurried into the foyer, feeling lighthearted and eager for what lay ahead. It was April and production plans for *The Chequered Silence* were on the move. A fine, clear April. The fur Cossack hat, winter coat and boots were replaced by a smart, perky pillbox and a three-quarter-length jacket in the latest style. As she walked into the hotel bar, Michael had a drink waiting for her.

'Contracts signed?' he asked, passing it over.

'They are,' Leah replied with satisfaction. 'Here's to *The Chequered Silence*,' and she raised her glass in toast.

'Here's to our angels—may they grow rich and multiply, and turn up in force today,' offered Michael dryly, 'or else there'll be no *Chequered Silence*!'

Leah pulled a face. 'I'll drink to that. Patty's coming round later with the brochures. Eliot can't make it. Do you think it will matter? He is an unknown, after all.'

'I think we have enough star names to impress,' said Michael.

'I only hope our director, whoever he is, isn't going to jib at his playwright being so closely connected with the production,' said Leah, 'but Eliot was so keen to be tutor for the sign language. I've pointed out that the director will have the final say on interpretation and Eliot says he knows that. I trust he does, when the time comes.'

'So do I, my dear, because you'll be sitting prettily in the middle if he doesn't,' observed Michael mildly, and Leah grinned. 'In any event,' Michael went on, 'I expect you can persuade Eliot Yates to do whatever you want.'

She allowed the remark to go unanswered and looked at him shrewdly, saying: 'You've been extremely reticent as to the name of our director.'

'Merely because nothing is settled yet and I don't want to bandy names until it is.' He hesitated. 'You found this play, Leah, and it's only right it should be yours, but it doesn't do to become too emotionally involved. You need just enough commitment to have faith in the play and transfer this first to the backers, which, I hope, we shall do today, and then to the director and the company. Anything beyond clouds judgment.'

Leah met this advice with a confident look. 'Don't worry, Michael. I can be as tough as the next man, if necessary.' She looked at her watch. 'I think we'd better go up. They should be coming presently.'

As the angels arrived, Leah ticked them off her list, and when all were accounted for, and the doors closed, she exchanged a satisfied glance with Michael.

She gazed round the assembled company, thinking, as always, what an odd and sometimes surprising assortment of people they were. Outwardly few appeared the type to invest their money in a theatrical venture. To be an angel, one needed to be a gambler, and the two maiden ladies from Northampton seemed an unlikely pair of gamblers. Yet, thought Leah, greeting them warmly, they were good for a possible three thousand. The staid-looking headmaster from

Hull—who would have supposed that he had unfulfilled ambitions for the stage which he satisfied by being an angel? He might come up with a thousand, speculated Leah, beckoning the waiter to refill his glass.

An accountant from Leeds, a hospital nursing officer from Plymouth, a housewife from Leicester—the list was long. All these people were small investors, but each person one of importance in a business where a hundred thousand pounds was required to put on a West End play. The big investors would be approached individually, but this motley crowd was just as valuable. Hence the five-star treatment.

Patty Turner arrived with the printed brochures which were passed round for the angels to read. The leaflets gave a synopsis of the play, information regarding the playwright, Leah herself as producer, and the actors taking the leads who were already cast.

Leah answered innumerable questions, working hard on the borderline cases, knowing her own enthusiasm to be persuasive.

When everyone appeared to have had their fill of the buffet food, and with the wine still flowing, Michael gave his usual informal speech, informative, flattering and amusing. He pointed out that *The Chequered Silence* was an exciting venture, one with which he felt sure they would eventually feel proud and thrilled to have been connected. He went on to say that Charles Raynor, an experienced and acclaimed actor-director, well known to them, had signed for the mature lead of the psychologist, and he was joined by Oliver Cape as the young male teacher. An unknown actress to West End audiences, Nancy

Holland, was playing the female lead. She was particularly well cast, being totally deaf herself.

This information brought a buzz of conversation from his listeners, and Michael waited a moment for the chatter to die down. He caught Leah's eye and a brow flickered and she gazed blandly back, but both of them knew that the overall feeling emanating from the angels was a promising one.

Michael began to speak again, announcing that he hoped to be able to introduce them to their director, an experienced man, both here and in other countries, possibly later on that afternoon. He asked for their patience, it would be rewarded.

Now it was Leah who felt some curiosity. Michael was being very mysterious, always a good ploy where angels were concerned, but she had a lively interest in the news herself. She gave a mental shrug. She would find out who the director was to be, sooner or later, and she trusted Michael implicitly in his choice.

It was to be sooner.

She was talking to the headmaster from Hull, when the door at the far end opened and a man paused on the threshold. His arrival caught Leah's attention and she took a step forward to investigate, then stopped short in her tracks.

'Oh, no!' she breathed. Fate could not be so capricious!

The man was tall and dressed in a sweater and cords, a jacket held in his hand, all in muted shades of brown. Assured, his eyes searched the room, and stopped briefly upon Leah's frozen form. With unchanging expression his search continued, finally resting on Michael.

The headmaster, seeing her face alter rapidly from astonishment to carefully controlled blankness, turned to look in the direction of her stare and asked curiously: 'Who's that, Miss Durrance?'

'Mmm...?' Leah dragged her eyes away and heard herself saying with amazing calmness: 'Max Calvert. He's the director Mr Walsh was talking about.' Her own appalled curiosity proved too much and she swung round again, watching Michael break away from the group of angels to whom he was talking and stride across the room to meet Max, who lifted a lazy hand in greeting and strolled towards him. They met in the centre of the room, shook hands and began to converse.

Leah's heart sank and she felt a sickening tightening in the pit of her stomach. Out of all the directors Michael could have chosen, he had to pick Max! Yet why not? She should have considered the possibility. Max was extraordinarily right for *The Chequered Silence*. It was a risky play, and he liked taking risks. He also had the artistic sensitivity that the play needed. Stepping outside her personal feelings, she could admit all that.

'Mr Walsh looks pleased,' observed the headmaster, and Leah pulled herself together and said confidently:

'Max Calvert is an exceptionally good director.' She took a sip of her drink. 'We're lucky to have him.' Lucky? Walsh Productions was lucky, whether Leah Durrance was remained to be seen. The angels sensed something important was happening and watched the two men with curiosity. Leah backed away, knowing she could not stay hidden indefinitely, but delaying the moment when she and Max had to meet.

From her safe vantage point she studied him. It was a little over a year since they had met at the Rosses' in New York and she had sensed a change in him then, but had not allowed herself the luxury of too long an appraisal. Now, taking her time, it was hard to define the change. He was still lean with an easy, indolent way of moving which in no way suggested slothfulness, but rather a contained and suppressed energy which she knew was released regularly on courts and in the gym. As she watched him talking to Michael, it came to her now that it was not only energy that was contained but the man inside the frame. At thirty-five, Max Calvert was even more his own person than he had been five years previously. The 'keep out' signs had been strengthened with time.

Leah saw Michael smile, a satisfied look on his face, and place a hand on Max's shoulder. He turned to his audience, his voice warm with pleasure.

'Ladies and gentlemen, I introduce you to our director—Max Calvert. His name is known to you, but I'll refresh your memories by reminding you of his most recent successes.' Michael reeled off a long, varied and impressive list, and his listeners nodded with approval and commented in under-tones between themselves. Michael waited a moment for silence, then went on: 'His past work speaks for itself, and we're extremely fortunate that Max Calvert has decided to join us. *The Chequered Silence* can only gain by such an association. Max, within the last hour, has stepped off the plane from the States, and I'm grateful that he's come along to meet you all.'

There was eager hand-clapping from the angels and Max smiled warily. Leah knew that smile. It meant—I know all this is necessary, but I wish I was out of it! Had he known she would be here? He had shown no surprise at seeing her, but Max had perfected the art of giving nothing away. She gave an impatient sigh. Here they were, the two of them, bound up in a situation where they were compelled to work closely together, with the utmost confidence in each other. The prospect was daunting.

'We seem to have come without a pen, Miss Durrance.'

Leah swung round and found the Northampton sisters smiling up at her. She found a pen and watched their cheque being made out. She caught her breath at the figure—four thousand! Bless them! They were twittering on about Max. They had seen some of his productions and knew how clever he was. Such an interesting man, and with a lovely voice and smile. Not handsome, exactly, but then they never trusted handsome men. What did Miss Durrance think?

Leah smiled. 'Come now, ladies, surely you know that *no* man is to be trusted!' and they giggled and signed the cheque. Leah watched them bustle their way to Michael, saw him make the introductions, Max stooping slightly to acknowledge their greetings. For the following twenty minutes Leah thought her smile would stay fixed on her face for ever as she enthused, encouraged and reassured. Gradually the angels began to leave, and Leah's panic grew. Without the angels she had no shield.

'We very nearly went off with your pen, Miss Durrance.' The sisters wanted to say goodbye. 'Mr Calvert was most charming.' 'He did look tired, poor man.' 'I wonder if he gets enough to eat?' The sisters took it in turn to speak and Leah made the appropriate replies. Max could still bring out the urge in women of all ages to mother him, she thought wryly ... which was a big laugh, for anyone less needing mothering was Max Calvert.

The room was emptying. The pile of cheques in Michael's hand looked rewarding. As she smiled and said goodbye, promising to keep in touch with production news, Leah was aware of that tall figure, now constantly watching her.

When the door swung to on the last angel, she took a deep, steadying breath, knowing she could not put off their confrontation any longer. She began to walk across the floor, both men watching her progress, but it was to Max she directed one fleeting glance. She shivered, her exposed skin feeling naked and cold, understanding her body in the way she remembered, almost as if his hands were already touching her.

And that's enough of that! she told herself fiercely, resolutely gathering together all her reserves and forcing herself to relax. Michael was smiling his self-satisfied, what-a-clever-chap-I-am smile. He put his arm companionably round her shoulders, turning to his colleague to say:

'Max, I want you to meet Leah Durrance, your producer. Don't let this soft, feminine look fool you. She can be as tough as old boots if necessary.'

Leah gave a laugh and held out her hand. 'I *think* that's a compliment! Hello, Max. How are you?'

Max nodded, his face deliberately bland, his voice polite.

'Hello, Leah,' and their hands touched.

'Of course, you have met, haven't you? Last year at the Rosses'. I forgot that Celia is your sister, Max,' confessed Michael, 'and tend to think of you and Henry as business associates rather than brothers-in-law.' He gave them both a benign look. 'Well, I need say no more. Good. That makes life easier, doesn't it?'

Leah clamped together her jaw, subduing the

spurt of hysterical laughter threatening to burst forth. Thumbing her nose at fate, she said:

'So Max turns out to be your surprise, Michael—what a feather in our cap!'

Max tilted his dark head at the compliment, a fleeting, ironic smile passing over his face. Michael grinned complacently.

'Thought you'd be pleased.' He looked at his watch and groaned. 'Lord, I have to dash! We've booked you in here, Max. Didn't know what your plans were, but I'm expecting you over at my place for the weekend, as arranged. Leah's coming, so she can pick you up on her way over.' He slapped the cheques into her hand. 'Here's the fruit of your labour, my dear. Get them into the office to be banked before they change their minds.' He swung round to Max and shook his hand enthusiastically. 'Very glad you decided for us, Max. Leah will look after you,' and on that barbed piece of information, Michael beamed at them both and strode off.

They listened to his footsteps retreating in the distance, heard him call out a farewell, which was followed by the noise of the banging door. They were now alone.

Hands laced together to still their movement, her lips moistened by the tip of her tongue, Leah said:

'This . . . has come as rather a surprise.'

Voice and countenance quite impassive, Max replied: 'Has it? I am only surprised that, working in the same profession, we haven't met more often.'

'I suppose you're right.' She looked at him uncertainly. 'When Michael contacted you regarding *The Chequered Silence* did he say I was the producer?'

'He thought he should mention that I'd be working for a woman.'

'He said my name specifically?'

'Yes.'

'And it didn't . . . put you off?'

'The play interested me. It would take a lot more than you to put me off an interesting play.' Gently sardonic, Max went on: 'On the other hand, I wasn't wild with excitement.'

'No,' Leah bit her lip, 'I don't suppose you were.' She glanced away for a moment and sought desperately for the right words. She was in an impossible position, one of professional authority over this man, yet he could make her job very difficult for her. She had to know where she stood with him. Her troubled green eyes came back to him.

'I want you to know that having someone of your experience and talent working with me on this play is an added bonus.' Because of inner tension the words came out stilted.

'A pretty speech,' Max acknowledged with a cynical incline of the head, brown eyes mocking, voice suddenly having a sting. 'It remains to be seen whether or not we shall be working together.'

Leah caught her breath, colour rising rapidly to her cheeks as she stared at him, searching his face, before saying sharply:

'I hope you're implying that you haven't yet made up your mind. If not, that sounded very much like a threat. I have every intention of working on this play, Max, I can assure you.'

He picked up one of the brochures from the table, studied it a second, then tossed it down. 'I would have expected you to be *in* the play, not producing it.'

'That's because you still think of me as an actress.'

He lifted his head, regarding her with intent

deliberation. 'Why aren't you?'

Evading the question, she told him defensively: 'It has been known for people to go from one side of the footlights to the other,' and he replied impatiently:

'But not you. Acting was your whole life. You were the last person to take such a step.' He paused and went on with pleasant malice: 'However, I never did know what went on inside that head of yours, did I? I thought we understood each other perfectly, but events proved me wrong.'

'I can do my job,' Leah said stubbornly, pushing the cheques still clutched in her hand into her handbag, dismayed by the underlying hostility in the outwardly composed face.

'So Walsh says, and at some length, and I should have thought him no fool. But then even the strongest of us can be fooled by a pretty face and winning ways. Walsh could prove no exception and be influenced by your prowess in other areas.'

As the words, spoken with silky offhandedness, penetrated, a wave of emotion swept over Leah, a mixture of hurt, shock and outrage, and the slap of her hand against his face sounded loud in the ensuing silence.

'That was a bloody minded thing to say!' she burst out angrily, and grabbing her wrists in a painful grasp, Max retaliated grimly:

'In this day of equality, slapping faces is a reciprocal gesture. Don't tempt me, Leah.'

'Equality! Don't make me laugh! Not when people like you automatically think that a woman has to sleep with a man before she can get anywhere!' She wrenched herself from his grip, rubbing her wrists, eyes sparking dangerously. 'Just because I jumped into your bed, you need not assume I make a habit of it. I've been working for Michael Walsh for over three years and the only influence I have, concerning work, I've earned through apprenticeship—damned hard apprenticeship. The fact that I'm a friend of his wife, and godmother to their children, makes your remarks even more offensive. I deeply resent them, on my own account and on Michael's.'

'You must put any reluctance I might have in accepting his word,' interjected Max witheringly, 'to past experience where you're concerned.'

White-faced, apart from two blazing spots of colour on her cheeks, Leah replied bitterly: 'No one walks out on Max Calvert without paying for it eventually, that's what you're really saying, isn't it? It must have been a blow to your pride if it still rankles after five years!'

It gave her great satisfaction to see dull colour come to his face, but his voice was unemotional. 'If we can keep this discussion on a purely professional level, leaving out personal issues, it would be more pertinent.'

'How can we?' she argued, in rapid undertones. 'That's a ridiculous thing to say! The minute you knew I was producer the whole thing took on a different aspect. I've earned this play, Max, and presumably you'd have no objection in the normal run of things to a woman being your producer. It's only because we were . . .' she stumbled incoherently over the words and he cut in suavely:

'Living together.'

'. . . involved personally, that you're being so foul.'

'Your reliability in the past hasn't given me a great deal of confidence.'

'I had every right to walk out on you, Max—we were not married, were we? As for walking out of

The Seagull, I'd signed no contract at the time and there was ample opportunity to find another actress, which you successfully did, didn't you? Alison Brett. No doubt she stepped into my place in your bed as well as into my shoes!' If she had hoped to goad him into any reaction to this reference of Alison, she was to be disappointed. Furious that her voice had become unsteady, she fought for composure, turning to pick up the scattered brochures, a snarl-up of conflicting emotions jumbled inside her. She made a great effort and went on more calmly: 'I apologise for that last remark. You're bringing me down to your level of thinking.' She drew an audible breath. 'Oh, I don't see the point in talking any more. You're obviously biased where I'm concerned. I can't altogether blame you, but you'll either have to take Michael's opinion as to my capabilities as a producer or back out yourself. I warn you, Max,' and she lifted long lashes, her eyes limpid and steady, 'I shall fight damned hard to remain the producer of this play. It's important to me, and I'm going to hang on to it. If you make things difficult, none of us gain anything and the play will suffer. You were sneering, a moment ago, when I spoke of your work, but I meant what I said. I've always had a great respect for you as a director.' She stopped, suddenly exhausted, wanting to end the interview. She glanced at her watch. 'I was planning on driving out to Churleigh about six, if that will suit?' She looked up, brows questioning. 'Unless you'd prefer to make your own way there? I can give you the directions.'

As if knowing that the last thing she wanted was a drive alone with him in the small confines of her Mini, Max said smoothly:

'My car isn't in London at the moment. Yes, I can be ready by six.'

Leah allowed none of her disappointment to show on her face, saying: 'Very well,' and walking to a chair, collected her coat, throwing it across her arm. She turned. 'Until six, then?' and began to walk to the door.

Max's voice stopped her. 'Could you let me have a copy of the play?'

She spun round slowly and stared in surprise. 'You haven't read it yet?'

'No.'

'You came all the way from America to direct a play you've not read?' The surprise was now in her voice.

Max lifted his brows, his tone dismissive. 'Walsh spoke to me on the telephone. There was no time to send the script over. He gave me a verbal summary of the play's theme. It sounded interesting. Walsh was enthusiastic. Where plays are concerned I have a healthy respect for his business and artistic sagacity.' He paused, adding, a sardonic twist to his mouth: 'It's only where you're concerned that I have my doubts.'

Leah tightened her lips. She said evenly: 'I'll have a script sent over immediately,' and taking a few steps nearer the door, hesitated. 'Have you luggage here with you? If so, I'll get it taken to your room.'

'It's at reception. There's no need to show how efficient you are, Leah—I'll take Walsh's word for that.'

Leah eyed him stonily, controlling her temper with difficulty. It did not now seem possible that this man's touch, the soft velvet of his voice, even the tread of his step had once caused the blood in her veins to sing.

She said: 'I always knew you could be a bastard, Max. I'll do my job, despite you. I'll be here at six,' and without waiting for a reply, she swung on her heel and left him.

Leah allowed herself enough time to get to the Savoy Hotel. As she drove through the Friday evening traffic she wondered what lay ahead of her this weekend. Nothing easy, that was certain. She had always known that the first real encounter with Max—and that brief meeting in New York could hardly count, with only two sentences exchanged and one frigid greeting—would not be an amicable one, but the real and the imaginary very rarely matched. Foolishly she had supposed, at the worst, indifference or even an outburst of healthy indignant anger. This cool, sardonic exterior hid a more hostile emotion, forcing her to look into the past through his eyes, something she rarely allowed herself to indulge in. She was also deeply troubled about her job, knowing that it was far easier for Michael to replace her than Max.

Coming down the Strand she swung into Savoy Court, pulling to a halt under the shining aluminium fascia, surmounted with the skirted and helmeted knight, of the Savoy Hotel. Max was there, ready and waiting, and opening the passenger door, swung a weekend case into the rear of the car before sliding his long length into the seat beside her.

As she inched her way out into the Strand again Leah said: 'Thank you for being so readily available. I think you'll find that your seat can go back a little more. I'm afraid these cars aren't made with the total comfort of six feet plus in mind.'

Max did as suggested, remarking: 'The Savoy approach must be the only place in England where you're allowed to drive on the right.'

'I understand it was decreed by Act of Parliament,' commented Leah. 'I do love that approach—with the hotel and theatre tucked away like that in typical London style. But then I love London.'

'Where are you living now?'

'I share a flat with a girl friend off the Bayswater Road.' She hesitated and went on diffidently: 'And you?'

'I still have my apartment in Eaton Square. A friend is using it at the present time.'

For one extraordinary moment Leah had the temptation to turn to him, as she used to do, and tease him about the word apartment, his American half lingering on the wrong side of the Atlantic. She only just stopped herself in time. As for Eaton Square—the less said about that, the better. Instead, she asked:

'Have you managed to read the play?'

Max moved to a more comfortable position, replying: 'Yes, I have.'

'Has it come up to your expectations?'

'Indeed it has . . . how did Walsh find it, do you know?'

'Michael didn't, I did. The playwright is a good friend of mine.' The minute she made the claim Leah wished it unsaid. It was an unnecessary piece of information.

Max made no comment other than a disinterested: 'I see,' and lapsed into silence, and the next time Leah glanced his way he was asleep.

'Thank goodness for that,' she muttered, and immediately found her tensed muscles relaxing.

Her mind was another matter. How strange it was, having him by her side after all these years, she thought; strange and unreal. She threw him another glance. He could not be very comfortable, curled up in that small area, arms hugging body, head resting cheek downward on the seat back. But then this capacity for instant sleep in the most awkward of positions was a knack to be remembered, along with such facts as that he loved home-made bread, French and Italian food, European cinema and astronomy and hated suet puddings and tripe and onions. That he was an avid reader, could speak fluent French and Spanish, was more than an accomplished piano player and usually slept on his right side.

And that's enough of that! Her eyes were drawn again to the recumbent figure. Dark lashes fanned across cheeks that were sallow tired. Unruly dark hair lay limp against his forehead.

Emotion lodged in her throat and she scowled fiercely, gripping the wheel hard and trying to empty her mind of everything but the feel of the car and the road ahead. She drove for some miles before giving up. It was no use. The figure by her side imposed his will, even asleep. It was incredible, she thought a little wildly, that by an odd quirk of fate they had been thrown together like this. Incredible and disturbing.

She changed gear and slowed for crossroads, then accelerated round a curve. Max shifted with the motion, one of his hands falling limply across his knee. Leah shivered. With bitter-sweet clarity she remembered the feel of his body lying heavy and hard against hers, the weight of his arm as they slept, the touch of his hand . . .

CHAPTER THREE

THEY had met in rather extraordinary circumstances. Leah was browsing in a second-hand bookshop situated in a narrow side street not far from the Charing Cross Road when an enormous spider dropped on to the open page of a book she was holding.

Arachnophobia is quite common, and the victims are not particularly proud of the fact that such a relatively small creature should scare the wits out of them. Leah was no exception, but that did not stop her from emitting, with all her force, a screech that rent the air and disrupted the calm of the other two occupants in the usually quiet and hallowed sanctuary of the bookshop. The screech was followed by the said book being flung high into the air and Leah putting as much space between her and the eight-legged object as possible.

The owner of the bookshop was in a small room off, drinking a cup of coffee and doing his accounts. The other occupant, on hearing Leah's screech, rushed round the centre division, met her coming the other way and caught hold of her, snapping: 'What's the matter?' The owner, having spilt coffee all over his paperwork, was hardly pleased when he heard Leah gasp:

'A spider!' She fought for breath. 'A huge ...' She gulped. 'It landed right on the book!'

Leah was, by now, beginning to feel a fool. Her head was buried in her rescuer's chest and she could feel the steady beat of his heart beneath her cheek, her hands clutching the rust-coloured shirt covering a hard rib-cage. When an amused voice said: 'A spider?' the inflection unsure that he had heard rightly, she lifted her head and replied indignantly: 'Yes—a spider! A bloody great spider! And I loathe and detest spiders!' A shudder ran through her. She extricated herself from his embrace and glared, daring him to laugh. 'It landed on the book,' she added, 'and might be there still.'

'If it is, then it's one hell of a pressed spider,' came the even more amused voice, 'but I doubt it's still there. The poor blighter was more likely scared silly by your yell and ran for its life.' He bent to pick up the book, examined it carefully, glancing at the shop-owner, who had now appeared on the scene, saying: 'The book is not damaged.'

'I want to buy it, in any event,' put in Leah quickly, and the owner nodded dourly and went back to his office. Leah eyed the book warily, her eyes dropping to the surrounds, searching.

'If it ran for its life, where, I wonder, is it now?' she murmured, sweeping hair from her face with an impatient hand.

'Why? Do you want to kill it?'

Her eyes flew to his, green eyes sparking. 'Good heavens, no! Why should I want to do that? Spiders are amazingly good creatures. I *never* kill them.' She scowled disarmingly. 'In fact, I go to extreme lengths to rescue the silly creatures. At least, not me exactly. I have to find someone to do that for me.'

His lips twitched, but he said gravely: 'I see.'

'I merely like to know *where* they are. It's their

sudden tactics that bother me.' She looked at him anxiously. 'You don't think it landed on me, do you? I couldn't bear that.' She stood rigid and slowly looked herself over. He put the book down and said kindly:

'Let me look.'

For the first time, Leah was able to regard him fully. Up to then she had had only fleeting impressions, but now, with his attention from her face, she could leisurely study his. And it was, without a doubt, in her opinion, the most interesting and compelling visage she had seen in a long time. Beautiful in its sculptured bones and chiselled nose, and ridiculously long lashes for a man. His eyes . . .

She found herself colouring vividly, for they were now connected with her own and were studying her quite openly. They were brown velvet eyes, and very, very expressive.

She was sure her face was as red as her blouse. What dastardly trick of fate had made her choose to wear her oldest, patched jeans today? And her hair! twisted into one thick plait down her back like a child, so that it would be wavy for that night. Her feet were thrust into sandals, leather thonged style, and a white cardigan was slung round her shoulders. This, her beautiful man was now removing, giving it a gentle shake and placing long-fingered hands on her arm to turn her round, which he did, Leah acutely conscious of his appraisal.

'No. No spider,' he said at last, and she breathed a sigh of relief and murmured:

'Thank you.' She picked the book up gingerly and feeling absurdly flustered, observed ruefully: 'Unfortunately, places like this attract them, don't they?' She found she could look at him again, feeling more in control. 'It was kind of you to come so nobly to my aid.'

'That's quite all right.' He smiled, fully and devastatingly, for the first time, and Leah was plagued by an aggravating memory hovering on the edge of her subconscious that she should know him. Was he an actor? she wondered. He had a way of sounding his vowels that was not wholly British, rather as though he spent, or had spent, a large part of his life in America. Whatever the reason, his voice was exceedingly attractive.

'Ellen Terry and Bernard Shaw, A Correspondence.' His gaze had gone to the title of her book. 'You're a fan of G.B.S.?' he asked.

'Some of him. He's rather wordy at times.'

He considered her for a few seconds before saying: 'By a coincidence I'm going to see *Arms and the Man* tonight. Would you like to come with me? It's opening night, but I'm sure I can come up with another ticket.'

Leah wanted to laugh, but kept her face straight. 'I should have loved to have gone with you,' she said, her voice regretful, 'but by another amazing coincidence, I'll be there myself. Perhaps I'll see you there?'

Their eyes met and held and Leah experienced a small tremor assault her senses, and she thought wildly: This is ridiculous!

'I sincerely hope so. I'll look out for you, unless,' and he paused, a brow winging upwards, '. . . unless you'll be with a jealous escort?'

'No,' Leah replied gravely. 'I shall be with a group of friends and none of them will be in the least jealous.'

'Tck, tck . . . I can hardly believe that.' Round

his mouth the curled lines deepened and the soft velvet of his eyes glittered. 'I look forward to seeing you afterwards. In the bar?'

'Thank you—I should like that.'

'We must hope that our eight-legged friends don't have a penchant for Mr Shaw's work.'

His lips parted into a lopsided smile, allowing a glimpse of white, gleaming teeth, and Leah found herself smiling widely back. She collected her wits and looked down at the book in her hands.

'I'd better go and pay for it.' Backing down the gangway of bookshelves, she added: 'Thanks again for coming to my rescue,' and by the time she had paid and the book had been parcelled up, the tall man had gone.

Two minutes before curtain Leah was sitting on stage, dressed in a voluminous white cotton nightgown with its beautiful broderie-Anglaise collar and cuffs edging the old-fashioned high neck and long sleeves. On top of this exquisite nightwear was an all-enveloping, shaggy fur cloak. She was ready to assume the role of Raina in George Bernard Shaw's play, *Arms and the Man*. She was wondering where her bookshop friend was sitting. That he was here, she knew, for some minutes before a packet had been handed in, brought by the theatre manager himself, with her name inscribed. Thanking him, she had waited until alone and had opened it with some curiosity, the title of a well-known jeweller's on the lid increasing her inquisitiveness. Resting on a bed of white velvet was an extremely pretty, delicately jewelled spider. The card merely read: 'Good luck. Maxim Calvert,' in black, flowing writing. The spider was now pinned to the inside of her nightgown where it would not catch the light, becoming an instant talisman.

Maxim Calvert—of course! Then she had remembered, at last, who he was. A man whose rise to the top ranks of theatrical directors had been built on exciting and dazzling productions, whose mere presence in the auditorium alone was worth a rapid pulse-beat and a spasm of nerves.

Leah suffered both, but only until the curtain rose and she had spoken her opening lines, and then no one counted, except Raina Petkoff, dreaming of romance in her bedchamber in a small town in Bulgaria in the year 1885.

The play went brilliantly. No one could put a foot wrong. The actors were enchanting and the audience enchanted. Laughter rippled through the theatre, rising and falling, to rise again and again, to end finally in thunderous applause.

Leah stalked into the bar and halted, her eyes moving slowly through the crowd of people, the hubbub of noise barely reaching her ears as she sought Max Calvert. She looked superb, a flush of excitement upon her cheeks, her slim body clad in an emerald green trouser suit of a flowing, silky material, styled on Russian Cossack lines. Her dark hair was drawn from her face in side wings and secured in a loose, deceivingly casual coil with a mother-of-pearl clasp. Her make-up was minimal and she moved in air touched by expensive French perfume. The effect was wholly for the purpose of erasing from Max Calvert's memory the flat-sandalled, jean-clad, pigtailed girl in the bookshop.

He was talking to some members of the cast already securing a position in the bar. His glance had strayed periodically during the past ten minutes towards the entrance, and now his vigilance was rewarded. For a moment green eyes met brown and then he was excusing himself from his fellows, threading his way through the crowd, unhurriedly, to meet her. Leah came halfway towards him, forcing her pace to be leisurely, glad of the one or two pauses for congratulations, knowing the colour was risen in her cheeks and heartbeat had quickened. This is only the second time you've met him—for sanity's sake, stop being a fool! she told herself scornfully, and hurriedly draped a mask of cool, sophistication to hide such foolishness.

They finally stood, a hand-clasp apart, and long, brown tapered fingers joined with her own, the brown eyes teased and the mouth softened into a faint smile. With a sigh of outgoing breath, Leah allowed the mask of cool sophistication to slip and said simply:

'I remembered who you were immediately I saw your name. I'm sorry. I'm afraid I'm more likely to know your actors. Unfair, isn't it?'

'Please! Don't apologise. *You* very nearly caught *me* out. I was sure I'd seen you somewhere before and came to the conclusion that it must have been on stage. I searched some recent stage magazines and found you, playing St Joan.' He shook his head slightly. 'How you managed to look such a plain Joan I'll never know. You have a quality of face that can subjugate whatever character you're playing—inherited, I suspect, from your famous mother.'

Pleasure, followed by a brief flicker of sadness, so swift that it might not have been, showed on Leah's face as she exclaimed:

'You surely were too young to have seen her!'

'Nuala Flynn? Oh, my dear, she captured my ten-year-old heart and held it for two years until she retired.' His voice had been lightly self-mocking but now softened with genuine kindness: 'The theatre lost a remarkable actress when your mother abandoned her profession.'

'She chose to be a wife and part-time mother instead.'

His brows rose. 'Part-time?'

Leah lifted a careless shoulder. 'I was an unlooked-for addition to the Durrance-Flynn alliance and as soon as was feasible, despatched to a suitable boarding school, where I worshipped both from afar.' Her voice was light and matter-of-fact. If there had been any soul-searching over this desertion it had been done long since. 'Neither the theatre nor I could keep Nuala Flynn from my father, Luke Durrance. They eventually died a rather nasty death together. I often wonder what she would have thought had she known her daughter was following in her footsteps.' She gave a rueful smile. 'If I have half her talent I shall be content.'

'My dear girl, from what I hear, read and see, you could eventually eclipse her.'

The praise, spoken in a level, cool voice, brought a shock of violent intensity to Leah, enveloping her emotionally. Her long dark lashes lowered quickly, to lie quivering for a long moment on hot, flushed cheeks before she gained control. Presently they rose, revealing a limpid steadiness, her lips only bearing witness by trembling slightly before saying:

'Thank you. I passionately hope you're right.' Her hand rose to the brooch on her shoulder. 'I also hope this is not wildly expensive...' She hesitated and he drawled:

'It pleased my eye and seemed appropriate—and

was a mere trifle. Has that absolved you of your
finer scruples?' and a dark brow winged upwards
while his eyes kindly teased.

Laughter escaped her lips as she replied
ingenuously: 'Indeed it has! Thank you, he's the
first spider I've wanted to keep.'

'Then I've been amply rewarded.' Max looked
round and went on with scandalised amusement.
'Do you realise that I've kept you talking for ten
minutes without offering you a drink?' He cupped
her silk-clad arm with his hand and began to draw
her through the crowd. 'I shall repair that dreadful
omission immediately and then, when you feel we
can decently depart, perhaps you will allow me to
feed you? I know most actors don't eat before a
performance. Are you hungry?'

'Famished!'

'Good. Then I shall introduce you to some
exquisite French cuisine and you shall tell me . . .'
he paused, his voice tinged with gentle mockery,
'. . . if, like Raina Petkoff, you're dreaming of a
noble and splendid hero, ready and willing to lay
down his honour and his life at your feet.'

'I can tell you now, Mr Calvert, that the only
thing I'm dreaming of is one day to see my name
up in lights,' and as she exchanged a glance of
matching rapier thrust, cards upon the table, Leah
Durrance and Max Calvert began their association
together that was to last a little under a year.

Leah had had no intention of falling in love with
him. She had never been able to take sex lightly
and although there was an immediate physical
attraction between them, their relationship progressed with decorum. They were both, at that
time, working in London and met regularly,
learning of their similarity in likes and dislikes,

their sense of the ridiculous and their love of their chosen profession.

As the weeks passed it became more and more obvious, though not voiced, in which direction their friendship could end. Leah judged Max to be holding back, wanting to lay down a solid foundation as to the rules of the game—marriage is for other people—before committing himself to a physical partnership, wanting no misunderstandings.

Leah was not totally inexperienced, but her work was a nomadic profession, relationships blossoming and then dying through lack of contact, and by the time she was twenty-three, acting was still the most important facet of her life and she had every intention of it remaining so.

Until Max ... and then she was plunged into loving him almost without realising it, knowing that anything that had gone before was dross. It frightened her, this emotion, even while it exhilarated and charmed her. She resented the hold Max had over her, knowing she was not a whole person any longer. It was necessary that he should not guess how deep her feelings had travelled, and she had to decide whether she was willing to submit herself to something that was bound to end in her being hurt. Unlike Max, she was not a cynic where marriage was concerned and had mentally written it on her itinerary, but it came below the 'name in lights'.

Fate stepped in, giving her a breathing space. Max's stepfather became ill and he flew to America to be with him. *Arms and the Man* had, by then, closed, and Leah was working at the Civic Theatre, Rotheringham, under the auspice of Charles Raynor. This separation, Leah thought stoutly, would prove something and make her come to a decision one way or the other.

It did. It proved that she missed him dreadfully.

The curtain came down one Saturday evening and Leah, taking off her make-up in the shared dressing room, heard a banging on the door and someone calling: 'Message for Leah Durrance— your bloke's in the bar waiting for you!'

When she walked into the bar, heart hammering, Max was with Charles. Leah paused, her eyes resting on him as he leaned casually against the bar counter, listening to the Rotheringham director. As if he sensed she was there, his eyes lifted to meet hers and their look held for a sensitive moment. Then she moved forward, controlling her features, aware of Charles's shrewd look at them both as she smiled in a friendly fashion and said easily:

'Hello, Max—this is unexpected. How are you? How's your father?'

Max replied: 'I'm fine, and Father's condition is at present stable,' and finishing his drink in one smooth movement, he took her arm and said to Charles: 'You don't mind if we rush off, do you, Charles? My time is limited.'

Charles looked from one to the other and smiled benignly.

'Not at all, Max. Just make sure she's back for a ten-thirty rehearsal Monday morning, will you?'

'Is this abduction?' Leah queried as Max put her into his Porsche, parked outside the theatre. She tilted him a glance, an uncertain smile on her lips, still not totally sure of his visit.

'It is,' was the calm reply. 'Which way to these digs of yours?'

'Turn left here.' She gave him an incredulous

look. 'Max, I know it's wretchedly out of date, but gentlemen callers are frowned on, and you'd hate the place, anyway, it's just not your style. I daren't upset my landlady, because digs in a university town are hard to come by . . .'

'I shouldn't dream of upsetting your landlady . . .'

'First right and then left.'

'. . . all we're doing is calling to pick up your toothbrush, and anything else you think you may need for a two-night stay away.' Max slowed the Porsche, pulling into a lay-by, finally stopping, but allowing the engine to run. He turned to face her, saying softly: 'That is . . . if you care to come.'

Leah said simply: 'Yes, please.'

His mouth relaxed. 'They say patience is a virtue. This past two weeks away has taught me that it's greatly overrated.' He leaned forward and kissed her, not touching her with his hands. 'It's been too long . . . much too long, and we've prevaricated enough. I've missed you, Leah. Have you missed me?'

She laughed softly, happiness spreading through her, and replied, gently teasing: 'You know I have.'

The brown eyes searched her face. Max said: 'Good,' and kissed her again, brief and hard, before driving off.

The hotel was quaint and quiet, situated by a river, and catered mostly for fishermen. Leah woke in the night, for a moment forgetting where she was. Memory came flooding back as Max turned in sleep and brought his arm across her, drawing her instinctively closer. It was just getting light. She could see his face and wondered if she would ever get used to the sight of his dark head on her pillow. He stirred and opened his eyes. Recognition came and he smiled lazily. His hand came up and smoothed the hair from her cheek.

'Can't you sleep?' he murmured, his eyes showing concern.

'I have slept,' Leah admitted softly, her lips curving, 'but it's not something I'm used to, sharing a bed with a large hunk of a man who's greedy for room.'

'I should think not, indeed!'

'You're right over my side,' she accused mildly.

Max laughed low in his throat, his eyes gleaming wickedly. 'Not surprising, is it? Even in sleep I'm drawn irrevocably to you.' He brushed his lips across hers and moved sensitive fingers across her smooth back. 'You'll have to push me away,' he drawled, his breath warm against her cheek.

Firmly encased in his arms, the length of her body by now moulded against his, Leah gave a deep sigh of contentment, her senses leaping to the intimacy of his touch, aware of a similar response in Max. The amazing thought came to her that perhaps the power was not one-sided! She shifted slightly and slid her arms round his neck, brushing her fingers upwards, combing his hair, and becoming voluntarily entangled.

'I guess I'll just have to get used to it,' she murmured, mocking his transatlantic drawl as she bent her lips to his shoulder, tracking kisses down the curve of his upper arm. She lifted her head, the look on his face making her add breathlessly: 'And . . . I don't believe I want to . . .' and then the words were cut off as his lips took hers and his hands became a language of their own.

Those self-same hands were the ones she could see now, brown, long-fingered with pale, nicely-rounded nails.

Leah's own grip on the Mini's steering wheel tightened and she scowled. Stop being so childish! she told herself furiously. What possible purpose has that bout of nostalgia served? It's no good looking back! But out of the corner of her eye she could still see Max's hand, illuminated by the dash.

The headlights picked up the turn-off to Churleigh and she swung the wheel over, easing her foot off the accelerator as she went down the narrow lane. There was within her a distinct reluctance to arrive, for she knew that some time during the weekend, Max would engineer a talk. There were still things to be said between them, their confrontation earlier in the day was merely the tip of the iceberg. At least, with him asleep and silent beside her now, she could pretend that this was an ordinary weekend with Ruth and Michael and the twins.

'Well, it isn't,' she muttered impatiently, 'and the sooner you get that into your thick head, the better,' and then the house came into view, roof and surrounding trees darkly outlined by moonlight.

She drove into the gravelled forecourt and stopped. Moving round slightly in her seat, she regarded him. Max slept neatly, his breathing and movement contained to a minimum. Leah said quietly: 'Max, we're here,' and touched his arm. His eyelids fluttered and opened. For an instant their eyes locked, suspended in a brief jump backwards in time, then the brown velvet turned to granite and he sat up, while Leah turned away, saying abruptly: 'We've arrived.'

Light streamed from the house as the front door opened and Ruth Walsh, a small, pretty brunette, came down the steps, followed by two spaniels.

She called a greeting and studied Max with open curiosity as he shook her hand and introduced himself, towering above her diminutive height. While Max was retrieving the cases from the car Ruth greeted Leah, kissing her cheek and giving her a hug.

'Lovely to see you! Come on in, both. Mind the dogs, they get under your feet if you're not careful, especially the pup.' She led the way in and spoke over her shoulder as they climbed the stairs. 'Michael is on the telephone, which surprises no one, but let's hope he'll be off the wretched instrument in time to eat. I'll show you to your rooms. You're in your usual, Leah,' and she stopped at the first door on the landing.

Leah took her case from Max, murmuring her thanks, and stepped into the room, hearing Ruth's voice continuing on as she pointed out to Max the bathroom, and then his own room. Mechanically she took off her coat and hung it in the wardrobe, listening for Ruth's return. She was opening up the case when the tap sounded on the door.

'Come on in,' Leah called, 'I want your opinion of this,' and she lifted out a dress from the top layer of clothing and shook it free of creases, holding it for Ruth to inspect. Ruth closed the door and voiced her approval, sitting on the end of the bed. They talked for some minutes, catching up on their respective news, then Ruth said thoughtfully:

'Michael says he's a good director.'

Leah did not need to know who ... there was only one director Michael was interested in at the moment. She swung the wardrobe door shut and said: 'He is. I've seen his work.'

'He looks a bit . . .' Ruth screwed up her face, struggling for the right words, '. . . formidable, until he smiles, then he's rather attractive. Shall you like working with him, Leah?'

'I . . . don't know whether it's all fixed yet, is it?'

'Michael seems to think it is.'

'Oh. Well then, yes, I'm sure I shall.'

'And you know him. That should help.'

'Yes. Although I've never worked with him before.' Leah placed her brush and comb on the dressing table, and resisted the impulse to tell Ruth just how well she knew him.

'He has a nice voice,' mused Ruth. 'Is he married? Michael, naturally, could only tell me about his theatrical history when I pumped him earlier.'

'Now, Ruth, will you stop trying to marry me off!'

Wide-eyed, Ruth insisted: 'Is he, though?'

'No, he is not married. He is, on the contrary, a confirmed bachelor. And however fascinating he might be,' Leah went on firmly, 'I'm not interested. I'm a career girl, remember? About to begin her first London production. I shall have enough problems without adding Max Calvert to them.'

'Phooey! That doesn't mean you have to behave like a nun!' proclaimed Ruth disgustedly. 'And I'll tell you this, my girl, nothing in this life is cut and dried. Take me—I'd no more intention of falling for the man of this house than flying to the moon . . . and if I'd known he was going to spend three-quarters of his waking hours on the telephone, I might have booked my seat on the rocket!'

Leah burst out laughing but would not be sidetracked. She said lightly: 'My dear Ruth, it's not policy to become entangled emotionally with one's director. In any case, Max Calvert is entangled already.'

'Oh? With whom?' asked Ruth, quickly interested.

'A woman called Stephanie Farrel, editor of a women's magazine ... or so Patty Turner was telling me this afternoon.'

Ruth shrugged. 'What a pity, but I suppose it was too much to expect him to be footloose. So he won't be giving Eliot Yates, and one or two others I could mention a run for their money?' she enquired mischievously. Leah gave her a half amused, half exasperated look and threw the play-script down on to the bed.

'*That* is where all my time and energy is going for the next few months,' she declared. Ruth picked up the script.

'Are you excited about it?' she asked, and Leah pulled a face.

'Excited, nervous, confident, worried—you name it, I feel it!'

Ruth grinned sympathetically. 'You should have seen Michael, the night you sent him home with it to read. I couldn't get him to come and eat. When he'd finished the last page he nearly drove me mad, walking up and down, cracking his knuckles in that infuriating habit of his. We spent the whole of the evening discussing the possibilities of production and staggered to bed in the early hours.'

'That's a nice thing to know,' rejoined Leah mildly, 'after I'd worked darned hard persuading him—he was poker-faced all through.' She paused, laying her nightdress on the bed. '*And* he got out of me far more than I intended to tell.' She looked at Ruth from under sweeping lashes. 'He told you, of course.' It was a statement rather than a question.

Ruth reached across and took her friend's hand in her own. 'It must have been a bad time for you, Leah. I wish we'd known you then. We could have helped.' She considered for a moment. 'It's strange how life takes on a different direction. You probably wouldn't be here now, ready to discuss the production of this play, would you?'

'No, but I might have been in it,' Leah returned soberly.

'You might, at that,' agreed Ruth. 'Does it bother you to talk about your deafness?'

Leah knitted her brows. 'Not really—although I tend to block out that period of my life . . . it was an unhappy time.'

'Michael thinks you should have told him—your fellow, I mean, but that's the macho male coming out in him. I can understand why you didn't, although it couldn't have been an easy decision to make or carry out.'

'It wasn't,' admitted Leah grimly, 'and Michael made me have enormous self-doubts for a while, for his views, though not expressed, were evident, but doubts are such pointless things to indulge in.' She snapped shut the empty case and swung it off the chair. 'It would be different if we had second sight—such as some of my Irish forebears are supposed to have enjoyed—that would make everything very easy, wouldn't it?' She put the case on the top of the wardrobe, adding dismissively: 'In any event, ours wasn't a permanent relationship. I knew that from the start. He . . . was not the marrying kind.'

'Hm. Another Max Calvert, eh?'

'You could say that,' agreed Leah, with ironic amusement. Ruth picked up the coffee-coloured nightdress admiringly, saying:

'This is slinky. Is it new?'

'Fairly, but not packed to impress the clever Mr Calvert.' Leah closed the last drawer.

'Pity,' observed Ruth, eyes twinkling, 'as he looks the type who'd appreciate it, too.'

'Without a doubt,' replied Leah dryly.

Ruth stood up. 'I must go and cast my eyes over the dinner. I told Mr Calvert to use the guest bathroom first, as he *doesn't* look the type who likes being kept waiting! He does, however, know how to get round a woman,' and she brought out a small packet from her pocket, brows raised. 'Chanel No. 5, no less—my favourite.'

Not Je Reveins, thought Leah, with a stupid pang of memory. Je Reveins was *her* perfume from Max, which she had been unable to wear for a long time because it reminded her too much of him. How ridiculous can you get! She said quickly:

'Very nice. Are Jenny and Gwilym asleep? May I have a peep?'

Ruth beamed a smile. 'Of course you may. They've been terrors today and sure to be fast off.' She paused at the door. 'Dinner in an hour and a half. Sherry or whatever in the library beforehand.'

It was just her luck that Leah should meet Max as she stepped from the bathroom, face shiny and hair limp from the steam. He was leaving his room, dressed in blazor and slacks, and both paused in their stride at the sight of each other. Max was the first to recover, giving her a short nod of acknowledgment before moving off down the stairs. Once in her room, Leah glared at herself in the mirror. 'What the hell! He's seen you without make-up before,' she muttered. 'You're going to work with the man, not seduce him!'

She put on the dress she had shown earlier to Ruth and, satisfied that her hair had regained its natural bounce, scrutinised herself carefully before leaving the room. When she walked into the library she was rather taken aback to find Max there, alone, and with some excuse already forming on her lips to make a retreat, since she was not ready for their talk together, he forestalled her by saying:

'Michael said to help ourselves. What can I get you?'

By the time the drink was poured Ruth and Michael had joined them and the danger was passed. Conversation turned to music, Ruth and Max both having an interest in the classical composers and both admitting to some expertise on the piano. When, eventually, they made their way to the dining room, Leah purposely allowed the other two to go on ahead, holding back so that she could ask Michael:

'Have you mentioned anything to Max about why I gave up acting?' Her tone was casual.

Michael replied: 'No. Do you want me to?'

Relief spread through her, making the first 'no' come out a little too forceful, and she went on more calmly: 'No, do you mind if you don't?'

Michael gave her a considering look and said reasonably: 'There's no need for him to be told. None of his business, is it?'

It took some doing to hold his gaze and say steadily: 'No, not really, although he'll know of my involvement with Eliot and TFTD.'

'I'll warn Ruth, though I doubt she would say anything in any event,' Michael assured her, and Leah murmured: 'Thanks. I'd rather he didn't know. Silly, but . . .' and she gave a light, shrugging laugh, not now meeting his eyes, disliking the evasive tactics she was using but considering that giving Michael the information that Max was the man she had once lived with would merely complicate an already complex affair.

That first evening was not quite the ordeal Leah had expected. Max seemed amenable to playing her game, one in which they were casual acquaintances only. Ruth and Michael were always good company and Max, with no apparent effort, added his own brand of wit and intelligence until he had them relaxed and often helpless with laughter, playing his own game with the hands of a maestro. Leah watched and listened, offering enough of herself to avoid comment, and was drawn, reluctantly, by the spell of his personality, to be charmed, soothed and seduced, holding back just enough, by sheer reason and self-preservation. Reluctantly, because the past can never be retrodden and Max Calvert was not a man to forgive lightly.

Ruth went to bed first, saying that the babies were early risers, and not long after, Leah made her own excuses. As she stood up to go, Michael said:

'We'll have a conference in the morning, Leah. Ten-thirty . . . all right?'

Leah said: 'Yes, of course,' adding a 'goodnight' to include them both. As she began to walk across the room she felt a stab of unease. Max, sprawling in a deep armchair, a glass of Michael's best brandy in his hand, rose to his feet and strolled ahead of her to the door, opening it with an indolent gesture. She murmured her thanks and he gave her a sudden malevolent smile before returning her a suave, uninflected 'Goodnight' as she passed him by.

Climbing the stairs, Leah determined to have all the facts at her fingertips the following morning. She would make sure that Max had no opportunity for criticism. She would show him that she was good at her job if it was the last thing she did!

CHAPTER FOUR

THE production meeting flowed smoothly and affectively. Michael kept in the background, interrupting now and again to clarify an issue or raise a query. Dates were arranged for auditions and actors' names were bandied about, some rejected, others noted down, to be contacted through their agents. It was decided that Nancy Holland, the deaf actress, was to have a special audition with Oliver Cape, who had been contacted again for that purpose. A photograph and details of her career were spread before Max and he agreed to give the final say when he had seen her in action.

Stage and lighting men and a set designer were next on the agenda and Max provided Leah with names of those he liked working with and she promised to find out if any of them were available.

Michael had not yet been able to contact the management of the King's Theatre so far, and in the event of it not being available in the autumn, as rumoured, other possible theatres were pondered over, Leah remaining firm in her belief that they should opt only for one that had installed a system for the hard of hearing, giving the proviso that, as a last resort, they would have to settle for one without.

Leah unrolled a wall chart she had constructed, a calendar of events through to September, on which she had marked a progress schedule showing advancement of the production of *The*

Chequered Silence. Publicity, rehearsal venue and budget costs—each was ticked from Leah's list, until finally the play itself was taken apart, discussed, and a general idea of direction was given by Max. Leah was not surprised by his grasp of the play in so short a time. It was what she expected of someone of his calibre. His cool, authoritative voice imparting his ideas tilted the final balance, showing her that any amount of personal anguish was worth suffering for *The Chequered Silence* to gain the talents of Max Calvert.

The morning passed amazingly quickly and they covered a great deal of ground. Leah could tell that Michael was pleased by the way things had gone and felt some satisfaction herself, although not for the world would she have shown it. Today had been all in a day's work and she would not look toward Max Calvert for a word of praise. At the end of the session Michael disappeared and beginning to sort through her papers on the desk, Leah, deciding attack was preferable to defence, said coolly:

'I gather you've decided to give me a chance.'

Max was standing at the window, looking out on to an expanse of lawn which dropped towards flowerbeds and the boundary hedge, beyond which lay fields and the spire of Churleigh Church. Towards the left was a small orchard and to the right, hidden from the house by trees, was a tennis court and summerhouse. It was a very English scene and the daffodils, tulips, the camellias and forsythia were splashes of colour among the fresh greenery. At her question Max turned, regarded her for a moment, and then replied:

'The play decided for me. Sorry if I've

disappointed you. I'm afraid you're stuck with me.'

Leah said tartly: 'I thought it was the other way around?'

He shrugged. 'Very well, we're stuck with each other.' He returned to his appraisal of the view. 'Have you told Michael about us?' By his tone he was barely interested.

'No. Have you?'

His head swung round at that and he gave an unpleasant smile. 'Hardly the kind of story I'd want spread around, is it?' He paused and went on smoothly: 'Why have you not married?'

Leah blinked; the question was totally un-expected and insultingly personal. A fine brow arched and she replied, sweetly antagonistic: 'It could be that no one has asked me.'

He looked at her with a sardonic gleam of comprehension in the dark depths of his eyes. 'It could,' he agreed, 'but I find that very difficult to believe. I'll retract the question. It is, as you are thinking, none of my damned business.' He inclined his head with an expression of courteous politeness, pausing a moment before adding dulcetly: 'Although I do feel I have a slight claim to interest. My successor obviously didn't come up to scratch.'

Leah's hands stilled on the papers and her head came up. She said carefully: 'Just what's that supposed to mean?'

Max lifted a negligent shoulder. 'You had every right to leave me, if that's what you wanted, but if you'd met someone else, why could you not have told me?'

In incredulous amazement, she demanded: 'What are you implying?' and then: 'There was no one!'

Max made no comment.

'I tell you there was no one else!' Indignation, turning rapidly to anger, made her voice rise. 'You needn't believe me, but it's the truth!' She searched his face for signs of belief and could find none in that chiselled, polite mask. She took an angry breath. 'Why should you suppose that? I told you in my letter . . .'

'Ah, yes, the letter. Propped up so un-imaginatively against the clock upon the mantel. Short and rather ambiguous, as I remember . . . but I do recall that there was a mention of a cooling off in our relationship.'

A dull red swept into Leah's face as she met his sardonic look of disbelief. She had defended herself, on writing that letter, that the explanation was the best she could produce that might be accepted as a sop to his pride. Those last few weeks had been difficult for both of them, for totally differing reasons. Owing to pressure of work Max was away often and when he did return was moody in a self-contained way, worried deeply over his father and desperately trying to rearrange his time-table so that he could fly over and see him. Leah was waiting for the results of the tests half knowing already what they were going to tell her. Had her life been normal she could have coped with the situation, made allowances, soothed and smoothed away the fears. As it was, she welcomed their uneasy alliance as part of a defence she knew she would need, and when a first-class row had developed, only minutes before he had to leave to catch the plane, regarding the actress Alison Brett, she flung herself into it heart and soul, the banging of the outer door as he left striking a symbolic note.

And now, it seemed, he had not accepted the sop to his pride, but had instead fabricated another man!

'If there had been someone else, I would have written so,' Leah ground out contemptuously, the green of her eyes vivid at the injustice. 'I can't imagine why you should think such a thing.' The flashing eyes interrogated and after a long pause, Max replied:

'I found your explanation difficult to accept. Another man was easier to believe.'

'Oh, yes, that I can well imagine!' she exclaimed, snapping the lock on the briefcase. 'Much easier to believe I'd walked out on you for another man than to think I'd grown tired of you! That wouldn't do at all, would it? I'm sorry for the way I left you, I knew at the time a letter was a cowardly way out, but I can't go on and on saying I'm sorry, can I? After all, it wasn't meant to last for ever, our affair, was it?'

The silence between them lengthened. Leah was quivering with fury. How dared he! How dared he think such a thing! Standing there, watching her, in that damned inscrutable way of his!

Into this tableau walked Ruth, heralded, fortunately, by one of the dogs, giving Leah time to turn away and busy herself at the desk and for Max to remove his gaze once more to the window. Ruth stopped short in the doorway, the silence and stillness of her guests hitting her in no uncertain manner. With her eyes going from one to the other, she murmured uncertainly:

'I'm sorry ... Michael said the meeting was over.'

Max turned and smiled, saying easily: 'So it is. I was admiring your garden.'

Reassured by his tone, Ruth joined him at the window. 'Yes, it's lovely in the spring, so clean and fresh.' She gave him an amused side glance. 'I wonder if you're aware that Michael intends to challenge you to a game of tennis this afternoon?'

Max's smile deepened. 'I'm quite amenable to the suggestion, but I haven't brought any kit with me.'

Ruth laughed. 'That's no problem. Michael can supply all shapes and sizes, excuses on that count are useless.' She addressed Leah. 'Will you come prowling this afternoon, Leah? I've heard there's quite a useful antique shop opened fairly near. We shall have to take the twins, I'm afraid, it's the girl's weekend off.' She turned back to Max, explaining: 'I have a young girl from the village to come in and help me most days, which is lovely. I love the little horrors, but they are a handful. Luckily, the twins have an extremely doting godmother who can be relied upon at times of stress,' and she smiled at Leah, who had gained control, and was able to answer lightly:

'They're darlings, and yes, I'd love to come with you.'

'Good. We shall be having a light lunch in about twenty minutes. Michael has promised to take us out for dinner tonight,' and giving her guests a bright smile, still unsure of what she had interrupted, Ruth summoned the dog and left the room.

'I'll come and help, Ruth,' Leah called after her, waiting until she heard Ruth reply: 'Fine,' and the sound of the door into the next room closing. Max was watching her. She demanded:

'Well? Do you believe me?'

'Does it matter?'

Leah stared, disgusted with herself because it did. She said flatly: 'You can think what you like,' and holding his look for a moment longer, turned on her heel and left him.

On the way home from their prowl, an antique writing case now triumphantly in her possession, Ruth said:

'Michael is pleased with the way this morning went. He said you were very efficient.'

The praise was warming. Leah replied: 'This part's easy, it's mostly planning and speculation.' She turned in the seat to check that the twins, sitting angelically in their car seats, were all right. 'We did manage to clear quite a bit of ground.'

'I didn't realise, until it was mentioned at lunch, that Max is related to Henry Ross.'

Leah stretched to pick up a toy Gwilym had dropped, giving it back to him and receiving a wide, toothy grin before he dropped it down again.

'That, young man, is enough of that!' Leah told him, before replying: 'Yes, Celia Ross is his stepsister.'

'Celia and Henry stayed with us the last time they were over here,' Ruth reflected. 'You were away, I seem to remember. Celia spoke of you. Said to tell you the next time you were in New York to be sure and look them up.' She paused to negotiate a tricky bend in the road. 'I think Michael hopes to interest Henry in *The Chequered Silence*.'

Leah's interest quickened. 'Really? For Broadway? That would be wonderful!'

'He's sending Henry the script, anyway,' Ruth confided, adding: 'So you might end up in America again, you never know.'

Leah murmured an appropriate reply, and wondered.

Michael took them to a nearby hotel for their evening meal. He and Ruth were in good spirits, emphasising the quietness of their guests, sitting, Leah thought crossly, like two zombies in the back of Michael's car. At the first opportunity of speaking privately with Max, she said:

'I realise spending the weekend in my company must be abhorrent to you, but do you think you could make the effort to look as though you're enjoying yourself? For Ruth's and Michael's sake?'

Max meticulously took her arm as they followed their friends into the dining room. Bending his dark head to hers, he replied smoothly:

'You're mistaken. Abhorrent isn't the word I would use. Intriguing, certainly curious, would more accurately pinpoint my feelings.' His eyes swept brazenly over her, bringing the first wash of colour to be painted on her pale cheeks. 'How could escorting a beautiful and desirable woman be abhorrent?' He drew her reluctant arm through his. 'However, you must practise what you preach. Should be easy enough—you haven't forgotten *how* to act, I presume? I'll direct you. Take a deep breath and relax, or you'll snap in half . . . and smile, even laugh at times, although we mustn't give Ruth Walsh too much encouragement. She has a matchmaking gleam in her eye when she regards us . . . which we both know is bizarre and doomed to fail.'

'You're the one who's mistaken,' said Leah, smiling as she had been bidden. 'Ruth knows that our interests, romantically, lie elsewhere.'

Max greeted this piece of information with a smile as pleasant as her own and they wound their way through the tables to where Ruth and Michael were now seated.

The grip on Leah's arm was firm and she was compelled to look as though this contact was not distasteful to her. She knew that they made an impressive picture as they stalked straight-backed and confident through the well-attended dining room. The difference in them was that hers was assumed. Max, bringing a breath of the States with him, was wearing a white tuxedo which with his height and distinctive chiselled looks made him the target of more than a few female eyes as they passed. Leah was fully aware of the envy afforded her in her escort by those discreet glances and knew that, in part, some of it was directed at her couture. A Kenzo creation in flowing silk, a mixture of riotous patterns of greens and blues, a Westernized influence on the Japanese kimono which rippled and shimmered as she moved, with long-legged grace, by his side. She wore her hair up and the light caught, and held, the string of emeralds hanging from her small, well-shaped ears.

What a romantic couple we make, she thought ironically, ignoring the swift thrust of anguish that suddenly pierced through her, and smiled again as Max pulled out a chair for her to be seated.

The meal progressed without incident until coffee was reached, when Ruth and Michael excused themselves and made for the dance floor. Leah watched them go, controlling her face, stilling the panic at the thought of being held in Max's arms under any pretext.

'They're a nice couple.' Max's voice was reflective. Relief made her respond warmly:

'Oh, they are, aren't they? I'm very fond of them both.'

'How did you meet?'

'I met Michael when I went to him for a job. I knew of him, of course. Ruth I met later. Their house is a second home to me.'

'And TFTD? How did you become involved with that?'

'Through Eliot Yates.' She lifted the coffee cup to her lips and drank, dark lashes lying composed on pale cheeks. She raised them and found he was observing her thoughtfully. 'I became interested in their work through him,' she told him calmly.

'Ah, yes—Eliot Yates. I can't say that I'm overjoyed at having our playwright breathing down my neck, however much we need a sign language expert.' His hands moved together and clasped themselves, lightly.

A shiver ran through her, a shaft of knowledge suppressed, to tease and taunt, a memory of leaping senses and gentle solace. She set her teeth, and said: 'He's a reasonable man. He's directed plays himself and knows the problems.'

'No playwright is reasonable, sitting in on the production of his own play. I hope you can control him, because if you can't, I shall.'

'You'll not be put to that trouble,' she returned, and Max drawled:

'You mean you have him securely under your thumb?'

Leah was saved making a reply by the return of Ruth and Michael. An interim lull followed and when the married couple once again took to the floor, Max rose to his feet, saying:

'I think we'd better dance, don't you?' and followed the suggestion with the wraith of a smile.

She rejoined instantly: 'I wouldn't dream of

putting you to so much effort, even in the call of duty.'

Max held out his hand, his voice soft. 'Not scared, are you, Leah?' His eyes challenged, and without another word she rose and walked stiffly, preceding him. At the edge of the dance floor she turned, green eyes limpid, face expressionless, and after a fractional hesitation, held up her hands.

They were silent throughout the dance, which was in a slow, dreamy rhythm. The dancing area was minuscule, no room for fancy steps, and Max's hold was necessarily an intimate one. Intimate yet impeccably impersonal.

This touching business was ridiculous, and the sooner she conquered it, the better. Leah could feel the warmth of his hand on her back through the thin material of her dress and in turn could recognise the touch of her fingers on the texture of the tuxedo, experience the cool lightness of his clasp on her hand, breathe in the mixture of their body smells, feel the brush of his face against her hair. Make of it what you will, mocked a horrid voice in her head, which she shut off with a vengeance.

When the music stopped Leah drew away and stood, her chin a little high, looking him straight in the eye. Max gave a dry:

'Thank you, Miss Durrance. That wasn't too difficult, was it?' and not long after they all left for Churleigh.

No one was talkative on the way back and after thanking Ruth and Michael for a lovely evening, Leah excused herself, making a general 'goodnight' and escaped to her room. Some minutes later Ruth tapped on her door, stepping rather diffidently inside on Leah's call. She said:

'I've left them swopping theatrical stories. Can you be a dear and undo this hook for me?' and as Leah went to help, she added: 'It's been a nice evening, hasn't it?'

Leah replied enthusiastically: 'Mmm ... yes, it has. Lovely meal.'

'I find, on closer acquaintance, that Max Calvert is a man one could come to like very much, if he ever allowed you close enough. Has that impregnable aloofness always been there, do you think ... or has it grown with age? He's intelligent, attractive in a sardonic way, bags of charm when he bothers to use it. I can't imagine him doing anything on the spur of the moment, can you?'

'There, that's done,' said Leah.

Ruth said, troubled: 'You are happy that Michael's given you the play, aren't you, Leah?'

'Of course I'm happy!' exclaimed Leah, scandalised. 'I'm thrilled to the core! If I'm not quite myself this weekend then it's because I don't want to make a fool of myself in front of the clever Mr Calvert.'

'You'll not do that,' retorted Ruth staunchly. 'Are you ... do you think you and he will get on together, Leah?'

'I have every intention that we shall,' declared Leah calmly, and Ruth beamed a relieved smile.

'Michael has the utmost confidence in you, remember that.' She kissed Leah's cheek. 'Goodnight, my dear. Sleep well,' and then she was gone.

Leah made ready for bed, her brain active. Impregnable—that was the word Ruth had used to describe Max, and yet no one was totally that. Some had a stronger wall to hide behind. It would be stupid to assume that merely because she had hurt his pride as long ago as five years, the hurt to self-esteem should be any less now. The fact that he was in a strong position to do her some hurt back was all that need occupy her. It was like a game of chess, a pastime they had often enjoyed together. Although a good player, Leah had never been the winner, but this time she was determined to win. *The Chequered Silence* was worth fighting for. So she would set out her chessboard and plan out her moves.

The problem was that not only was she fighting Max, but herself as well. Max was no more the same person of five years ago than she was, no one stays the same, and the difficulty, if she were to be honest with herself, was that although her head told her this, her senses told her something else. What had attracted her to Max then attracted her now, which was ridiculous and self-deluding ... and hopeless.

And Eliot? What of Eliot? Though she had not allowed him to voice it, Eliot wanted to marry her and she had even been toying with the idea, lately, of saying 'yes' to him. She was twenty-eight and the years were passing quickly, too quickly. Her work was deeply satisfying, but she would like to believe that there was someone, somewhere, with whom she could share the rest of her life, share the raising of a family.

Max, either from a hint from Michael, or using his own intuitiveness, had cast Eliot as the King on her chessboard and it was up to her to defend him. Eliot had no share in their battle.

She was returning to her room on the way from the bathroom when she faltered in her step at the sight of Max coming slowly up the stairs towards her. His head was down and she didn't think he had seen her as she quickly slipped into the room and very gently closed the door. Feeling a little foolish, she crossed to the dressing-table and began to brush her hair. A knock, and then another, sounded on the door and she half-turned, brushing suspended, knowing who it was. Before she could do or say anything, the door swung open and he sauntered in, jacketless, the ends of his tie hanging loose. He stood for a moment taking in the softly lit bedroom and the girl, standing motionless, arm raised with brush in hand, the light throwing shadows on the curves and hollows of a slim body that the coffee-coloured nightdress did nothing to hide.

Leah caught her breath, found her voice and demanded: 'What do you want, Max?'

He raised dark mocking brows. 'What would you say, my dear Leah, if I answered "you"?' and he nudged the door with the heel of his foot until it clicked shut.

'I'd say you've got one hell of a nerve and I wouldn't believe you,' she replied, red staining her cheeks, as she put down the brush and quickly collected the matching robe which she had tossed across the back of the chair.

'A little late in the day for modesty, isn't it, Leah?'

The malevolent taunt deepened the red and she tried the robe round her waist feeling vulnerably exposed. She attacked coldly:

'You're drunk—you've indulged in too much of Michael's best brandy. Get out, Max. Your right to enter my room like this ended a long time ago.'

'I haven't forgotten.' He walked slowly towards her. 'And I'm not drunk. Pleasantly mellow, perhaps, but perfectly capable of knowing which is my bedroom door and which is yours.' He stopped an arm's reach away and allowed his eyes to travel slowly the length of her body and back again. 'A pity—you're very desirable. The pretty girl has grown into a beautiful woman.' His hand came up to take her chin between thumb and forefinger, forcing her to meet his gaze. 'You have the most expressive eyes. At the moment outraged indignation is sparkling in their fiery green depths.' His lips curved. 'You'd really like to create a rumpus, wouldn't you? But you can't, can you? No good running to Michael—that wouldn't do at all. You're supposed to be the capable Miss Durrance. In any event, what would you say? We're old friends, after all. I merely came in for a chat—for old times' sake.'

Leah jerked her head away and said with knife-edged control: 'We have nothing to talk about.'

'Oh, I wouldn't say that,' he protested mildly. 'I've come to the conclusion that there's a great deal to talk over. But not tonight.' His eyes narrowed as he observed her expression. 'And I'm not going to rape you, either—I like my women complaisant. On the other hand, I think you owe me this——' and cupping the back of her neck, he pulled her to him, kissing her with bruising force and contemptuous disdain. It did not take long. When he let her go, Leah staggered back against the dressing-table, one hand supporting her trembling body, the other shielding her lips. Eyes hooded, face unreadable, Max went on: 'Primarily, I came to return this,' and he dipped his hand into his pocket and dropped something on to the table top where it spun for a moment, glittering in the light. 'I found it on the stairs. It hasn't much monetary value, I know, but since you've kept it, it has perhaps some sentimental value. I'll bid you goodnight,' and turning on his heel he walked steadily to the door, opened it, gave her one last thoughtful look, then closed it gently behind him.

Leah had not realised she was holding her breath until she released it in one long sigh. Sinking to the chair, she stared at the wide-eyed image before her, flushed and brightly glowing, tears of anger trembling on the ends of her lashes. She tentatively moistened her lips with the tip of her tongue. 'Damn him,' she muttered without emphasis, and moving swiftly to the bedside table wetted a piece of cotton wool with water from a jug, left there by Ruth earlier. The ice in the vacuum had not melted totally and the water was cold. Leah renewed the procedure a few times and decided, with a little luck, she would pass muster the next day.

First move to Max, she thought grimly, and yet he had allowed her one small advantage. He still thought her desirable. Her eyes caught the glitter of jewels and pensively she stretched out her hand and touched the spider with a tentative finger. The safety catch had broken; she would have to get it mended. Max was quite right, it did have sentimental value and she would not like to lose it. And Max could make of that what he wished!

'Wow! Come and have a look at this!'

Leah obediently put down the Sunday paper and joined Ruth at the window. 'This' was a white sports car which had swept up the drive and out of which now climbed a well-dressed, extremely attractive blonde.

'I wonder who she is?' murmured Ruth curiously. 'Did Michael say he was expecting anyone down today?'

'Not to me,' admitted Leah. Ruth left the room and Leah returned to her chair. She had not slept very well and felt less than her usual self. She had met Max on the stairs earlier and he had stopped, saying abruptly:

'I hurt you last night. I apologise.'

She had replied with tremendous composure: 'What's a few bruises between . . . old friends? If it gave you satisfaction . . .'

'It didn't.'

That had been the full extent of their conversation together so far that day. The door re-opened and Ruth returned, her eyes bright with knowledge, the blonde at her heels.

'This is Stephanie Farrel, come to collect Max. Miss Farrel, Leah Durrance, a friend and colleague of ours. Do sit down while I go and see if I can find Max for you. He and my husband disappeared after breakfast. I rather think they're playing trains.' She smiled and left the room.

'Trains?' Stephanie Farrel stared after Ruth, then turned finely shaped brows to Leah. 'Did I hear Mrs Walsh say "trains"?'

Leah replied politely: 'You did, Miss Farrel. Do please sit down. Yes, trains . . . Michael builds them. It's his hobby. He has a large workshop and layout in the attics.'

'Really? How fascinating!' Stephanie Farrel gave a small, secret smile, followed by a delighted chuckle. 'Somehow, Max and toy trains don't seem to go together.' She draped herself elegantly into a nearby chair, looking round the room appreciatively. 'This is a lovely house, and in such a pretty rural area—not so far from London as to make the journey unacceptable. Do you live in Churleigh, Miss Durrance?'

'No—London. I'm a weekend visitor too.' Leah bent to stroke the spaniel pup who had just padded in and placed himself against her legs, his mother already lying contentedly on the rug.

'I've heard of Walsh Productions, but I've never met its owner. Max has spoken of him. You work for Michael Walsh?' Stephanie asked.

'I'm one of his producers,' Leah replied politely.

'How interesting. There can't be many women producers around?'

'More now than there used to be,' admitted Leah, and Stephanie stared at her thoughtfully.

'Tell me what you do, exactly. Most people outside the theatre get confused between the definition of director and producer.' She gave a smile. 'I really am interested.'

'A producer does the administrative work,' Leah explained. 'Casting, choosing staff, finding a theatre, keeping costs within budget—making everyone happy.' She allowed herself a wry smile. 'That's not easy sometimes.'

'No, I shouldn't imagine it is,' acknowledged Stephanie, prompting: 'And the director?'

'He deals with the artistic side of the production, the interpretation, the mood, and he has final say on the set and costume designs, music and lighting.'

'In other words—Max,' offered Stephanie. She thought for a moment and came to a decision. 'Miss Durrance, I work for a magazine called *Woman's View*—you may know of it? Would you be prepared to come along and give us an interview? Explain your job? I'm sure our readers would find it both interesting and informative.' She broke off as the door opened, exclaiming warmly: 'Max darling, how well you look! Lovely to see you.'

Max, moving in his easy, relaxed way, walked across the room and took her outstretched hand, smiling down at her. There was something in the gesture and the look in Stephanie's eyes that spoke volumes. Leah recognised it and so did Ruth, coming in behind Max. Leah's feelings were mixed ... but one of them was certainly relief. A footloose and fancy-free Max might have gone to her head, and that would have been self-destructive. There was no future in which Max was involved, other than professionally, and to think otherwise was foolish.

Ruth was irrationally disappointed. Despite all the odds, she had quite made up her mind that Max Calvert would do for Leah. This Stephanie Farrel was a formidable stumbling block. Michael came forward to be introduced and the usual small talk ensued for a short time, until Stephanie turned to Max, saying:

'I'm trying to persuade Miss Durrance to let me interview her for the magazine. Don't you think she'll make a good story? A perfect example of a woman in what used to be a male-orientated profession.' She threw a droll look in Leah's direction. '*Do* you have problems being a woman in your job, Miss Durrance?' she asked provocatively.

Leah looked across the room at her. Max was now sitting on the arm of Stephanie's chair. They made an attractive picture.

'Sometimes,' she admitted coolly, 'but usually not for long, not once it's realised that I can do my job just as well as a man.'

'You'll have to ask Max what he thinks of women producers, Miss Farrel,' suggested Michael, his face deadpan, and Stephanie swivelled her head to Max enquiringly, and he obliged with an equable:

'Miss Durrance is producing my next play.'

Stephanie gave a gurgle of laughter. 'Really? Then I shall certainly ask Max,' she acknowledged to the room in general. 'I might even persuade him to be interviewed with you, Miss Durrance.'

'Wouldn't be a bad idea,' conceded Michael. 'Good advance publicity. Battle of the sexes angle.'

'Michael dear, Max and Leah aren't going into battle, surely?' protested Ruth, and Michael replied promptly:

'Definitely not! I have the utmost faith in my producer,' and everyong laughed, Leah's sounding rather hollow in her own ears, and she found her eyes drawn back to Max, who raised an ironical brow. She said quickly: 'May I give you a ring later, Miss Farrel?' and Stephanie nodded, bringing a card from her handbag, saying:

'I'll not let the idea drop too easily, it's a good one. I'm sure our readers will be delighted to learn how you keep directors like Max firmly under your thumb!' and she shot Max a sly smile, receiving a slow, lazy one in return.

'Will you stay and have a meal with us?' asked Ruth hospitably, and Stephanie gave a rueful glance at Max before refusing with attractive regret.

'Do you mind awfully if I say no? This wretched man has been in the States for the past month and he promised to wine and dine me tonight to catch up on all our news, and I'm holding him to it,' and again she glanced at Max, giving him an intimate, half-questioning message.

Max said: 'Thanks, Ruth, but we'd better be off.

Perhaps another time? Excuse me while I fetch my things.'

On his departure, Leah allowed the others to dominate the conversation and found herself studying Miss Farrel with a great deal of curiosity. Good figure, expensively and tastefully dressed, attractive in a slightly hard, elegant way. Blonde hair smooth and styled, make-up impeccable. A career woman, but there was no concealing her confidence where Max was concerned.

During the goodbyes, Stephanie gave a persuasive: 'I do hope you'll say "yes" to an interview, Miss Durrance,' while Max slanted her a glance, giving an offhand: 'I'll be in touch,' and then they were gone. As the white car moved down the drive Ruth remarked pensively:

'I wonder how serious that is?' and Michael, sitting heavily down into an armchair and rescuing part of the newspaper from beneath the dog, replied dryly:

'Mighty serious, by the way she shot him away. Couldn't wait, could she? I doubt Max'll catch up on his jet-lag tonight.'

'Oh, really, that's all you men think about!' protested Ruth crossly, and her husband eyed her over the newspaper.

'You don't think it's news they're going to catch up on, do you, lovely?' he asked, and smiling, he went back to his reading.

Ruth pulled a face, laughed reluctantly, and went out of the room. Leah tried to concentrate on her half of the paper, but the words were a jumble. She let it fall and lay back, her eyes closed. *She* was a jumble. She felt fragmented, like a jigsaw puzzle, where none of the pieces seemed to fit . . . and she didn't like the feeling at all. For over three years her life had been mapped out before her—a West End production of her own the goal. Now she was nearly there and Max Calvert could ruin it all for her, in more ways than one, if she let him.

'Any problems, Leah?'

She opened her eyes quickly and smiled. 'Why, no, Michael.'

'You were frowning,' he explained mildly. 'If you do have any, come to me with them, won't you? That's what I'm here for,' he added, his attention already back to the paper.

'Yes, of course,' murmured Leah, 'but there's nothing I can't handle.' She picked up Stephanie Farrel's card and studied it. Apart from the printed address and telephone number of the magazine's offices, there was an inked insertion at the bottom. Leah stared at it, the whole of her body still. It was Max's Eaton Square number.

She stood and stretched. 'I think I'll take the dogs for a walk.'

Tramping across the fields, the dogs racing ahead of her, Leah wondered if her confidence had been misplaced. A week ago she had thought there was nothing she could not handle, but that was before Max had walked in on the scene. She gritted her teeth and gave a determined swing at the wayside grass with the stick she was carrying. She had stood on her own two feet far too long to go crying to Michael for help. And in any case, there was nothing Michael could do.

It was really up to her. And Max.

CHAPTER FIVE

UNA Bell was late, but that, acknowledged Leah, was nothing new. She idly scanned the busy Charing Cross Road from her window seat, the menu for midday lunches lying unopened in her hand. She was content to wait. She had liked watching people, ever since being a child. She would watch and wonder and pretend, and create warm, loving families out of the unknown faces. On the deaths of her parents, when she was really and truly on her own, those fantasies ceased, but not the watching. Now her keen eye was only interested in the walk, the stance; her ear on the accent, the inflection . . . and habit dies hard.

It was June and the weather was giving decided hints of a warm dry spell—men were in their shirts, sleeves rolled high, and women were in gay cottons, legs and arms bare to the sun.

A face leaped out from the anonymous crowd and her meandering gaze took a jolt, her attention caught and held. It was Max. He was walking on the opposite side of the road, his height and stride making him stand out amongst his fellows. In a few seconds he turned into the Underground station and disappeared from view.

Leah poured out a glass of water and took a drink, her face pensive. She resumed her inspection of the busy street with unseeing eyes, thinking back over the last few weeks, Since that dreadful weekend she and Max had contrived an easy truce, never alone together, and *The Chequered Silence* their common denominator. The first major setback had been the unavailability of the King's Theatre until the spring. Leah had been called into Michael's office to hear this news, Max already being there. They had discussed other theatres, with Leah holding out for one with facilities for the hard of hearing, and Max had said:

'There isn't one empty in the autumn, and to wait for the King's is impractical.'

Leah, sick with disappointment, and knowing he was right, glared, before turning to Michael. 'Couldn't we do our pre-opening in Nottingham, as planned, then take the play on tour, bringing it to London in the spring?' she demanded.

'Rather putting the cart before the horse, isn't it?' intervened Max, and swinging round, Leah said sharply:

'Well, what do you suggest?'

'Take whatever theatre is available.'

'Compromise, in other words.'

'Life is all one compromise,' Max drawled, and Leah, cheeks flushed, replied:

'With any play but this, I'd agree with you.'

Michael, sitting thoughtfully at his desk listening to them, broke in, saying: 'There is one way out—unorthodox, but it could work.' He had their attention, and sinking down into a nearby chair, Leah heard him say: 'We could open on Broadway first,' her excitement rising, and she repeated:

'Broadway? Would the unions allow it?'

'The unions on both sides of the Atlantic are endeavouring to co-operate more,' Max observed, giving Michael a speculative appraisal as he sat down on the remaining chair, leaning back and crossing his legs. 'You've been doing your homework, obviously. Is Henry Ross in on this?'

Michael nodded. 'I sent him a copy of the play a few weeks ago and he was very interested and wanted first option on our taking it over there. I was speaking to him on the phone and happened to mention our problem. He suggested we look into the possibility of opening on Broadway with a limited season for the English company, an American cast going into rehearsal to take over, at which stage the English company would come back home and open in London. The fact that we would only be playing for a limited time, probably eight weeks, with the American company taking over, would ease things with the unions.' He cocked them a questioning look. 'Well? What do you think?'

'What theatre can he offer us?' asked Leah. 'Will it have Sennheiser installed?'

Michael grinned. 'The John Golden—and yes, it does have Sennheiser.'

'It's worth looking into,' commented Max.

'I agree,' said Leah, 'but we must make sure of the King's for the London opening.'

'See what I mean?' Michael asked of Max. 'As determined as they come!'

'I've never doubted her determination,' Max said.

Suddenly Leah caught sight of Una Bell emerging from the Underground, and her thoughts turned from that recent meeting in Michael's office to the loyalty of her friend and erstwhile agent. Una had stood by her, solid as a rock, not offering advice but lending a sympathetic ear, and when Leah had finally come to the decision to leave Max, had helped her carry it through. Now, those days and nights spent alone while Max was in America, not eating, refusing to answer the telephone or the door bell, swamped in a welter of misery and despair, seemed unreal. She could look back and feel a certain amount of impatience with the girl she had been then, even knowing she was too hard on herself. And she had pulled herself out of it, hadn't she? All the weeping and wailing had been pure self-indulgence, for she had known she had no choice but to leave him. Una, a persistent finger on the door bell, had walked in when that decision had finally been reached and had taken over. She had found Leah a bed-sitter, kept in touch, and later visited her in hospital. Yes, Leah thought fondly, Una was a good friend.

Una now hurried through the restaurant and heaved herself into the seat opposite, dumping her parcels and bags under the table, breathing heavily.

'Greetings. Sorry I'm late. What are you having?' and pushing back her iron-grey hair from a hot, flushed face, Una relaxed her ample girth and picked up the menu.

When their order had been taken Una sat back, eyeing her young friend with approval, noting the fashionable red and white polka-dot dress, the bright red sandals, the clear-eyed, healthy gaze.

'Don't need to ask how you are—you're looking terrific. Having your own Broadway show obviously suits you. How's things?'

'Hectic,' answered Leah, smiling, 'but I'm loving every minute of it.'

'Good. I've just seen your illustrious director getting on the tube, as I was leaving it. Doesn't alter much, does he?' and Una's voice added grudgingly: 'He's got talent, I'll give him that,' as if that was all she would allow him.

'Yes, he has talent,' agreed Leah, fully aware of

her friend's bias. She leaned her elbow on the table
and rested her chin on her hand, going on
persuasively: 'Let me tell you what he did on the
first day of rehearsal. When everyone arrived he
handed out to each person a pair of ear-muffs and
told them to put them on, excluding, naturally,
Nancy Holland and Ann King, her understudy.
Then he sat them down in a circle and began to
talk. He went on for a quarter of an hour solid—I
wasn't there, Ann told me—and then indicated
that they could take the muffs off. By this time
they'd realised what he wanted to put over—the
isolation of being deaf. It turned out he'd done the
same thing himself, for a whole day, as an
experiment, to find out what it was like. Of course
Nancy and Ann, from then on, think he can do no
wrong.'

'Ann is partially deaf, isn't she?' interrupted
Una, and Leah nodded.

'Yes. She wears an aid. She teaches at the
Mission, along with Eliot. She can lip-read and
do hand-sign, and will stand in for Eliot at
rehearsals when he can't be there, as well as
understudy Nancy. Nancy, on the other hand,
has been deaf from birth and can't speak.
They're both good actresses and are working
hard with Oliver ... and as I've said, would
work all day and night as well if Max asked
them.' She raised a brow at Una. 'But don't you
think that was an amazing thing to do on the
first day of rehearsal?' she asked, refusing to be
sidetracked.

'Clever,' agreed Una.

'You should watch him at work. His observa-
tions and ideas are really inventive. The play is
going slowly and it's hard work at the moment,

but Max is making it grow, bit by bit—it's fascinating.'

'Hm ... is it the play that's fascinating, or the man? I always thought part of your trouble was hero-worship.'

Leah made a laughing disclaimer, but there was a shrewdness in Una's observation that was very close to the truth. She had been a little in awe of Max in those early days and with the advent of her disability it meant that she was less than perfect. Had she subconsciously considered that only the perfect was good enough for Max?

Their meal arrived, and Leah said: 'Your girl's coming along nicely, Una,' referring to one of Una's actresses who had a small part in the play.

'She's not a bad little thing,' agreed Una. 'Did Calvert know she was from my agency when you cast her?'

Fork halfway to her mouth, Leah frowned. 'I don't know. Why should...?' She stopped and lowered the fork, her food forgotten. 'Good heavens, Una, don't tell me he boycotted your agency after I'd left him?' It was the producer's job to cast, but no producer would willingly cast someone about whom his director voiced objections.

Una flapped her hands. 'No, no, the other way around. I don't think for one moment Calvert would have been so petty. No, I steered clear of him. In any event, he seemed to work more in the States than over here during that period, didn't he? The once or twice I've bumped into him he's been polite, but I never get the impression I'm one of his favourite people.' Una pulled a grimace of a smile. 'You can hardly blame the man. I was your agent and refused him access to your address—

can't expect him to forget that. No one likes a witness to a loss of dignity, and to a man like Max Calvert, who seems always in such command of himself and his destiny, it couldn't have been easy to come to me in the first place.'

Leah looked at her with increasing consternation, saying helplessly: 'Una, I didn't realise.'

'And when he did come, my goodness, was he formidable! All cold politeness on the outside and a seething volcanic mass on the in! I even found myself feeling sorry for the poor fool until I remembered that the man was an idiot for not marrying you in the first place and then he wouldn't have lost you. I don't hold with all this airy-fairy living together,' Una said flatly. 'The minute something difficult comes along the relationship splinters. You'd not have gone if you'd been married to him, would you? No, of course you wouldn't. You'd have weathered it together. He deserved to lose you.'

'Now, Una,' reproved Leah, smiling, 'you know I wasn't ready for marriage at that time. What! Give up my career like my mother had? Not likely! It only dawned on me too late that perhaps, with the right man, you could combine marriage and a career. Anyway, I'm sorry you had to put up with some repercussions.'

'Don't be ... I'm more than a match for the Max Calverts in this world. So! It's all finalised for a Broadway opening, eh?'

'Very nearly. Nothing else should stop the contracts being signed. We shall do our week at Nottingham and fly to the States, rehearse a week over there and open at the John Golden Theatre.' Leah grimaced. 'Each time I say the word "Broadway" I shiver!'

'Calvert, with his experience of working over there, should be an asset.' Una paused. 'I take it that things have eased since you've told him why you left him.' As her question remained unanswered and a telltale blush rose to Leah's cheeks, Una stared suspiciously and exclaimed: 'Leah! *Have* you told him?'

'No, and before you ask "why not" I'll say I don't know,' Leah replied stubbornly. 'No, that's not true. I do have reasons, but none that sound sensible and have everything to do with pride. I just don't want him to know, that's all.' She gave an exasperated laugh. 'There's no need. It doesn't alter anything, either in the past, or now, does it? It's over and finished.'

There was a long silence and then Una said gently: 'But, my dear, the trouble is, I don't think for one moment that it is.'

Leah felt her colour deepen beneath Una's kindly gaze. 'You can't imagine we can pick up where we left off, Una, just by my telling him,' she argued, and her lips curved derisively. 'Someone called Stephanie Farrel would strongly contest that—and so would Max. I'm not on his list of favourite people, either.'

'Don't suppose you are,' acknowledged Una amiably. 'You hurt the man's ego, didn't you?'

'And it would be foolish to suppose I was in his thoughts for long,' said Leah. 'He was never one to waste his time and energy on something over which he had no control.'

'He would dislike that, of course,' observed Una thoughtfully. 'Calvert would dislike not being in control.'

'And we're neither of us the same people we were five years ago,' stated Leah calmly.

'True.' Una studied her. 'I don't know about Calvert, but you have changed and gained in the process. You've matured and become more self-confident. I wish you'd not given up acting. I allowed you to overrule my better judgment. Yes, I know you'd lost your nerve and it would have been difficult, and it's good that you're making a success of this new career of yours, but I still have a hankering to see you treading the boards again. You thought by closing the door on acting you'd close it on Calvert as well. You need to exorcise the man, once and for all. Why don't you go to bed with him? He's sure to try and get you there eventually. That might solve all your problems.'

'Really, Una,' protested a laughing Leah, 'No one would suppose you to be a perfectly respectable granny! I thought you didn't approve of such goings on?' and then: 'Why on earth do you think he'll do that, when he can't stand the sight of me?'

'To remind you of what you threw away?'

'What an old cynic you are,' teased Leah, after a split second's pause. 'I'm sorry to disappoint you. I never allow myself to bed my director—it leads to complications,'

Una held the green, wide-eyed gaze and then gave an unladylike snort. 'Hm! How does Eliot Yates get on with Calvert?'

'Like a house on fire.'

'You sound disappointed.'

Leah groaned a laugh. 'Oh, lord, do I? How awful! I'm not, truly. Eliot's merely fallen under Max's spell, like everyone else.'

'We've agreed he's a good director,' Una pointed out mildly.

'Yes, we have.' Leah paused for thought. 'Eliot's

vulnerable, this play is so important to him. I'm glad things are going smoothly between them, naturally it makes life much easier for me, but I must admit to wondering, at times, why it is going so smoothly.' She raised her eyes expressively and shrugged. 'I can't explain.'

'I suspect the main problem is watching one's ex-lover becoming a buddy with one's present lover, when really you'd prefer them to be fighting a duel.'

'Una, you're incorrigible!' burst out Leah, giggling, adding after a moment, 'but there's a horrible amount of truth in what you say!'

The rehearsal room was the first floor of a warehouse which gave off an attractive aroma of the spices which were stored below. Accoustically it was not brilliant, but it was light and reasonably situated. Leah had known worse. As she opened the street door, about to ascend the wooden stairs, she heard clattering footsteps coming down and as the stairs were narrow she waited at the bottom until she could have a clear passage. The figure that came into view was Eliot. He beamed a smile on seeing her, exclaiming with pleasure:

'Leah! I thought I'd have to miss you—what excellent timing. Come and have coffee with me before I dash back to school.' He took her arm and persuaded her out into the sunshine. Leah hesitated, checked her watch, then smiled, saying:

'Very well, but I can't be long,' and Eliot, propelling her along the street, replied cheerfully:

'Neither can I, but we'll not let that worry us. Here, this will do. Not quite the Ritz, but what tourists call quaint.' He pushed open the café door and ushered her in and when they found a table, ordered two coffees, then went on regretfully: 'I never seem to see you these days.'

Leah teased: 'It's all in a good cause, isn't it?'

Eliot grinned. 'I still can't believe it, even after all these weeks! *The Chequered Silence* actually in rehearsal—unfolding, just as I'd planned it in my head, before my eyes.' He pointed a finger. 'But that doesn't mean I can't moan.'

'Poor Eliot, you're going to moan some more,' warned Leah, as the coffee arrived. 'I can't make tomorrow, I'm afraid. I have to go to Nottingham.'

Eliot gave a dramatic sigh. 'I thought I'd be seeing *more* of you. I suppose I do, really, but you're always wearing your producer's hat.' He gave a quick, reassuring smile. 'I do understand, don't look so worried. Drink your coffee.' He sat back and gazed at her appreciatively. 'You're looking beautifully cool. I don't know how you do it in this heatwave. We've not had a June like this in years, have we?'

They talked, mostly about the progress of the play, until Eliot caught sight of the time and went to pay the bill. Leah watched him go, feeling suddenly low in spirits. Anyone would be proud to be loved by Eliot, she told herself, a little desperately. Intelligent, articulate, with a good sense of fun. He was attractive, with laughing blue eyes and tawny hair. Patient too—perhaps that was the trouble, and yet she didn't want to be hustled either. She didn't know what she wanted, Leah thought, exasperated, that was the problem!

Coffee paid for, she joined Eliot and together they walked back to the rehearsal building.

'Are you pleased with the way the play is going?' she asked, and Eliot nodded, darting her an odd, guarded look.

'Max is working them hard. I've never seen such total commitment from actors before. And on my play. Makes me feel a bit awed.' He grinned. 'And scared too. Did you know that Max is learning hand-sign? Ann is teaching him. He asked her to.'

Ann had kept that to herself, thought Leah, but made no comment. She stopped in the doorway. 'I'm sorry about tomorrow night, Eliot. I promise we'll have a night out together as soon as possible. I have been sitting in on rehearsals, though, so we're not totally cut off.'

'I'm grateful for small mercies. Even if I can't talk to you I can look at you.' Eliot drew her into the doorway. 'I'll take advantage of this small amount of privacy. There—that will have to keep me going for a while. Take care, Leah,' and touching her cheek gently with his hand, he turned and left her.

Leah stood still, analysing her feelings, the pressure of his lips still on hers, then she climbed the stairs and opened the top door. She slipped quietly inside, not wishing to attract any attention and disturb the concentration and flow of the performance, and sat on a bench just by the door, taking stock of what was going on.

Despite her care she had been observed entering and one or two people acknowledged her presence with a smile or a lift of the hand. The twosome engaged in dialogue in the middle of the floor took no notice of anyone or anything going on around them other than themselves. Neither did Max, straddling a chair, leaning chin on hands, face intent, as he watched them.

Leah schooled her features, assuming an analytical appraisal of the trio, but it was Max who drew her eye.

His outline, sideways on, was sharply defined, standing out in relief against the pale cream wash of the wall. Dark hair, cut shorter than normal for coolness, lay in damp waves, giving shape to his skull. The long forehead was smooth, the eyebrows straight with concentration, and the eyes, deep-set, were half hidden with drooping lids, frilled top and bottom with fine, brush-like lashes. The nose jutted, predominating the profile, but was compensated by the smooth, shadowed hollow of flesh stretching from the cheekbone to the strong jawline. The mouth seemed to go down slightly at the corner, taking its cue from two deep scores, one from the nose, the other valleying the cheek.

So much for the head. Eyes travelling downwards, the navy T-shirt fitted tautly across a hunched shoulder and back, and a muscular arm, bent at the elbow, was tanned and covered with fine brown hair. Hands were balled, supporting the jaw, and the deep cleft between mouth and chin was occasionally explored by an absently moving thumb. The curved arch of the spine seemed out of proportion, split in half by an expanse of smooth brown skin gaping between navy cotton and belted trousers in faded denim. A long, lean leg was bent sharply at the knee, the thigh pulling at the seam, and the total posture was balanced on the ball of a foot which was clad in soft leather moccasin. If it was possible to look relaxed and taut at the same time, thought Leah, an uncontrollable ache searing her throat, then that was Max, at this moment.

Damn, damn, damn, she ground out inside her head and dragged her eyes away from him to stare, with the utmost concentration, at the two actors.

Oliver, dark and Slavonic-looking, and Nancy, blue-eyed and slender, with body movement like a dancer and expressive, long-fingered hands. Leah sat quietly assessing their performance. It was, in her opinion, good, and even at this stage, deeply moving. Oliver had worked hard. His sign language was very nearly perfect, but he had set himself a high standard and often his hands would go up in the air in exasperation when he made a mistake, as he did now. Ann, Leah's flatmate, darted forward, going over the phrase that Oliver had not mastered.

The rehearsal picked up again where it had left off. The fans made a whirling sound, high up on the ceiling, but even with their help, the room was still warm. By the time Max called a halt everyone was feeling tired, hot and sticky.

Charles Raynor wandered over to speak to Leah, greeting her warmly with: 'Leah, my dear girl, come to keep an eye on us?'

'Of course.' Leah made room for him on the bench and thought once more how lucky they were to have tempted Charles away from Rotheringham. She had worked for him, and with him, in the past and admired him both as a man and as a performer. She had felt a personal sense of achievement when he accepted to play a role in *The Chequered Silence*. His physical appearance alone was worth a great deal. Charles was a tall man, hair once fair was now silver-grey and lay in thick waves across a well-shaped head. He had compelling blue eyes and a Roman nose, a beautifully resonant voice and a strong stage presence.

'How do you think it's going, Charles?' asked Leah, and he pursed his lips, replying:

'I'm always wary of passing judgment on plays I'm involved with personally, but I have a tingling in my toes about this one, although the public is capricious in deciding what it likes. Young Nancy will steal everyone's heart; it was a stroke of genius on your part to cast a girl who really is deaf. And Oliver will give his best performance yet.' He gave her a side glance. 'You could have a hit.'

'I hope so. We do have a strong cast,' said Leah.

'And an excellent director.' His eyes left her and were now upon Max, giving instructions to Nancy and Oliver. Ann was translating Max's words in hand-sign to Nancy who, with Oliver, was listening intently. A close-knit foursome, while all around them was the bustle of the rest of the company getting ready to leave.

'I must admit I was mildly surprised to find that Max was directing,' went on Charles, his blue eyes guileless.

Leah took a breath, fumbling for the right words. 'Charles, about Max and me ... I want to tell you that it wasn't Max's fault ... that we split up, I mean. I wouldn't want you to think ... I want you to know that it was all my doing. I ... er ... finished our relationship.'

Charles said kindly: 'I'm sorry, Leah. I thought you were well suited. I'm disappointed to have been proved wrong.'

'Yes, well—I'm afraid I upped and went,' she said lightly, trying to be cool and knowing the colour was rising in her cheeks.

Charles murmured: 'Did you, indeed? Poor chap.'

'I just wanted you to know,' Leah said lamely.

Charles, smoothing fingers along an immaculately trousered leg, reflected: 'It would appear that your "upping and going" coincided with your disappearance from the stage.' It was a statement with the hint of a question in its depths. Leah was saved from prevaricating by the arrival of Ann, her impish face bubbling with laughter from something Oliver had said, asking:

'Are you coming home straightaway, Leah? Or shall I wait?'

Leah shook her head. 'No, you go, Ann. I shall be a while yet.'

Ann smiled and said goodnight, linking up with some backstage people on the way out.

'That was nothing to do with Max,' Leah said urgently, in an undertone to Charles, 'my leaving the stage.'

Nancy and Oliver paused in their going, Oliver lifting his sweat-stained shirt away from his body and grimacing distastefully.

'We're on the way to the pub to put back some of the liquid we've lost,' he joked. 'Coming?'

'Not tonight, dear boy,' replied Charles, and Leah shook her head, smiling her refusal. Nancy signed goodnight and they moved off together.

'Nothing at all to do with Max, Charles,' Leah repeated, looking at him anxiously.

He turned his face to hers, giving her his full attention for the first time since this conversation had begun. 'I don't want to pry, Leah,' he told her gently, 'but when you dropped out of *The Seagull* I rather jumped to the conclusion that you'd refused to work with Max.'

Leah frowned and said slowly: 'I lost my nerve.'

The silence stretched between them until Charles commented:

'It does happen. A pity. The profession lost a fine actress, wouldn't you agree, Max?'

Leah's head swung round. Making no noise in the soft shoes he was wearing, Max was standing barely an arm's reach away. His thumbs were hooked into his belt and he was staring down at the floorboards.

He raised his head at Charles's question and regarded Leah, an odd expression on his face, then replied almost absently:

'Yes—yes, it did.'

'But gained an excellent producer,' added Charles, patting her arm paternally. He rose to his feet, saying a trifle wearily: 'I must be off.'

Leah said diffidently: 'There are a few things I want to go over with you, Max. Can you spare the time now?'

Max rubbed a hand through his hair and nodded, reaching down for a can of beer in a cooling box, popping the lid and holding his head back as he poured the liquid down his throat.

Charles, picking up his things, admonished: 'Don't work too hard. Goodnight, both.'

When the door closed behind him, Max stopped drinking and eyeing her thoughtfully, stated: 'So— you lost your nerve.'

Leah replied a brief: 'Yes,' and walked to the table where she began to sort through some papers, withdrawing from a folder the ones she wanted. Max tossed the empty can into a waste-bin and strolled over to the table, leaning his hands on the two edges either side of a corner, looking down at her work.

Leah began to explain and discuss each point at issue in a methodical and precise manner. She was aware that he was watching her with unwarranted deliberation and began to feel the familiar tightening in her gut, which in turn made her angry with herself, the whole combination of emotions being covered by a terseness of voice and manner. She could see, out of the corner of her eye, his hand curved round the table edge, the tanned forearm, the watch at his wrist with its wide leather strap. It was with a sense of relief that she began to deal with the last points on her list, saying crisply:

'I have here the biographies for the Nottingham programme and subsequently for the John Golden. I've checked everyone's but yours. Do you think you could look through it and see if the dates and information are correct?' She handed him the paper and their fingers touched, briefly. Max straightened and crossed to a chair, concentrating on the contents.

Leah followed suit, choosing a chair on the opposite side of the table, moving without energy. She pulled the restricting band from her hair and shook her head, shaking the length of hair free. She was sitting beneath one of the fans and leaning back, closed her eyes, enjoying the breeze on her face and bare arms. The whirling of the fans was soothing, backed by the distant noise of the traffic in the street below. With sudden awareness, Leah realised that this was the first time that she and Max had been totally alone for some weeks.

She opened her eyes and straightened her back, to find that he had finished reading and was watching her.

CHAPTER SIX

'Is it correct?' Leah asked, and Max replied absently: 'Mmm? Oh, yes, it appears to be,' and skimmed the paper negligently across the table top.

She waited a moment, every nerve shrieking awareness of their isolation in the large, empty rehearsal room, then went on: 'Is there anything in particular you want me to ask the Nottingham people?'

'Nothing I can think of.'

'If there is, you'll be able to contact me through Patty at the office. I'll leave a number with her.' She smoothed a strand of hair from her face. She wanted to go but forced herself to appear unhurried, saying: 'That's all, I think.'

His head came up at that, and he looked at her as though seeing her properly for the first time since the beginning of their conversation. 'Not quite all,' he stated casually.

'Oh?' Leah raised her brows questioningly. 'Something bothering you?'

The pondering expression cleared and he eyed her blandly, stretching out his legs as if preparing to stay some time. Leaning back and linking his fingers behind his head, at ease and totally relaxed, Max replied laconically: 'Yes—you.'

Head high, sustaining the long, steady look, she said carefully:

'What exactly do you mean? Are you dissatisfied with my work?'

He gave a short laugh which ended on a long-drawn-out sigh, his hands coming down to hang loosely by his side. 'Hardly. All this is efficiency epitomised,' and he wafted a hand at the papers on the table.

'I'm very glad to hear it,' rejoined Leah a shade tartly. 'You'd be the first to complain if things were not run smoothly.'

'You're damn right, I would,' he agreed mildly.

'Then if it's nothing to do with production, perhaps it can wait? It's getting late . . .'

'I didn't say it was nothing to do with work. You're shooting off to Nottingham and I won't get you alone again for some time. You've been to a great deal of trouble during the past few weeks to make sure that we're never alone, you and I. Your policy being safety in numbers.' His lazy eyes challenged her.

Truth is a difficult thing to deny under such a stare. Leah said stiffly: 'All the problems we've come up against have involved, usually, someone else who needed to be in on the discussion. If you wanted a private talk you should have asked for one.'

'I'm asking for one now.'

Leah rose to her feet and moved to the drinks machine, jabbing the Coke button and pushing in a coin. Watching the cup being filled, she said: 'Very well.' She brought the rim to her lips, back still turned to him, and took a long drink. It was not very cold, but it was liquid and her throat desperately needed some help. She pivoted slowly, adding: 'Fire away.'

'Are you going to marry Eliot?'

Although his tone was flippant, his eyes, Leah noted, were not amused and never dropped from her own. The question was so far from what she had been expecting that she nearly choked on the drink. Taking a deep breath, she firmed her lips, looked briefly away, and then re-addressed him, coolly defensive. 'I really can't imagine why you're interested.'

'Can't you?' He lifted a shoulder. 'I'm asking a simple question. You need not answer it if you don't want to.'

'A very personal one,' Leah squashed the paper cup and dropped it into the waste-bin, 'and I can't see that it has any bearing on the production.'

'Indirectly everything to do with each of us has a bearing, but I'll come back to that later.' He paused. 'Are you?'

'If and when I decide to marry Eliot, I'll let you know.' She moved in to the table and began to clear her papers, aware that Max was rising and walking slowly round, to hitch himself on to the corner closest to her. It was a relaxed, easy manoeuvre which had placed himself squarely between her and the door.

'He's a nice guy, Eliot. I'm not too sure of him as a playwright, though. I suspect he's put everything he's got into this play and will struggle to find anything more to say, but I might be wrong. Has he asked you to marry him?'

Her eyes speaking volumes, Leah replied a level: 'No.'

Max nodded, undaunted by either the look or tone, or by the fact that she was thrusting papers into the briefcase with an obvious intention to finish and go.

'That's because he knows you're havering— what a lovely word that is! one that my Northern ancestors are fond of. No man springs a question like that unless he's pretty sure of the answer. So it'll be up to you whether he asks you or not.'

'Really? You sound very knowledgeable.'

'It could work, I guess. Eliot's in the same business—always an advantage. He'll be sure to accept the odd hours and estrangements with more tolerance than an outsider. As I've said, he's a nice guy—I like him . . .'

'I'm sure, when he realises that, it will make his day.'

'. . . but I'm not so sure he's the man for you. You'll tie him up in knots and run rings round him. Getting your own way will satisfy you for a while, but eventually it'll begin to pall. Too bland a diet becomes boring after a while.'

'How kind of you to be so concerned,' ground out Leah between her teeth, smiling.

'Besides, he's not really in love with you,' Max went on conversationally, having her full attention with that outrageous statement. 'He's mixing love with gratitude. You waved your magic wand and—hey presto! his play is being produced on Broadway, all because of Leah Durrance. I'm not denying . . .'

'Max Calvert! I am not . . .'

'. . . the fact that you'd be easy for Eliot to fall in love with.'

'. . . in the least bit . . .'

'He's bedazzled with you. But he's not in love with you.'

'. . . interested in your views!' Her voice was shaking with anger. She snapped the lock on the case and clenched her fingers round the handle to stop them trembling.

'I could be wrong,' Max acknowledged, his tone belying his words.

'How magnanimous of you!' Bright, flashing green eyes swept him a contemptuous glance. 'Whether I marry Eliot or not has nothing to do with you.' She swung on her heel, intending to put as much space between herself and this insufferable man, when she was halted by his hand, shooting out to grasp her wrist.

'Some weeks ago I'd have agreed with you,' he asserted suavely, 'but not now. Now I know you'll be short-changing the poor guy.'

After one movement to free herself, Leah subsided and stood, stiff-legged and backed, all the colour was leaving her face. As green eyes challenged brown, she said at last: 'What do you mean by that?'

His grip still firm on her wrist, his voice cool and calm, Max replied: 'You'll be settling for a compromise, merely for the security of marriage. You'll be opting for safety. As for Eliot, he probably won't realise what's going on until it's too late, but it's Ann who you'll really be hurting.'

The fans whirled steadily in the ensuing silence. Leah stared into his face, anger being displaced by shocked uncertainty. His eyes were very dark and totally unreadable, as was his expression.

'Ann?' she questioned at last, and Max inclined his head, freeing her wrist. She rubbed it abstractedly with her other hand as she said flatly: 'Why do you say that?' and swinging away from him, sat down on her recently vacated chair, face and body averted.

'Because Eliot's really in love with Ann King and she with him.' Max folded his arms across his chest, regarding her rigid back, her pale face. 'She's a nice girl, Ann, and very fond and loyal where you're concerned. She's known Eliot for a few years, hasn't she? Long before you came on the scene, and I suspect that if you hadn't . . .' He left the sentence unfinished and waited while Leah assimilated what he had said.

Presently, Leah asked: 'Has Ann told you?'

'About how she feels for Eliot? Not directly, but we've talked, mostly when she's been teaching me sign language—told me more, perhaps, than she's realised. And I've watched her when she thinks she's unobserved. I'm not mistaken about Ann, believe me. And I'm almost sure about Eliot, who, poor fool, is in a muddle. Therefore, my dear Leah, if you have no intention of saying "yes" to Eliot, I would suggest you give him the old heave-ho.'

Ann in love with Eliot? Leah wanted to pour scorn upon Max's assertion, but there was a small part of her that hesitated.

'You know, you've confirmed what I suspected,' Max was saying. 'If you really loved Eliot you'd be telling me to go to hell—and Ann too—that all's fair in love and war, as the old adage goes.'

Her head swung round and she said defiantly: 'What makes you think I won't say just that?' and then: 'And what did you mean—that I was short-changing him?'

'Ah! That brings us back to you—and me,' he answered ruminatively, and Leah said coldly:

'There *is* no you and me.'

A sudden, malevolent smile curved his lips. 'So you've told me once before.' The smile vanished, although the voice remained pleasant. 'Then why,' and he slowly lifted a hand and ran a finger lightly down her bare arm, 'if there is no you and me, do you jump like a scalded cat when I touch you? Why the tenseness, the brisk manner, just for my benefit? I seem to have a peculiar effect on you, Leah, and I'm extremely curious to know why.'

On a shattered breath, Leah said: 'Yes, well, stay curious.'

'You admit I'm not imagining it?'

'I'm not admitting anything! Can't you get it into your thick head that perhaps I might be impervious to your charms? Must every female fall to the ground in worship?'

Silkily, he said: 'Hell, no, that would be most inconvenient, and not at all likely.'

'Leave me alone, Max. Isn't Miss Farrel enough for you to handle?'

His eyelids flickered. 'I've told you, I've tried to ignore your attitude towards me, but you've made it impossible for me to do so.'

'If I have an ... attitude, it's understandable, surely? I've had to prove myself to you. I'll even admit to the very normal human failing of wanting to impress you,' and on this note of impatience she shot him a baleful glance, rising abruptly and stretching for the briefcase which Max now moved out of reach.

'I'll accept that,' he answered reasonably, 'for the first few weeks of working together, but it must have been apparent even to you that any reservations I might have had at the beginning were soon dispelled by your proficiency. I've been admirably served by my producer, and if you were not aware of my relief and subsequent confidence in your efficiency then you must be singularly obtuse—or wilfully stubborn.' He paused. 'The first I doubt, the latter, is possible.'

The praise, more valuable for the matter-of-fact way in which it was given, brought a small patch of colour to her face and totally disarmed her for a moment, cautiousness again taking over when he went on:

'It was in April when we first began to work together. It's now June. Nearly twelve weeks. If you were like it with everyone, I'd merely take it that efficiency had fossilised all the warmth and zany love of life you used to have. But ... the brittle smile, the brisk voice is for me alone—and it's making me nervous.' He gave a lazy smile. 'There must be a reason.'

Rejecting swiftly a number of half-formed replies, Leah finally said: 'I think you're exaggerating,' voice and countenance guarded.

The fringed lids dropped over Max's eyes. 'I'm not, you know. Others have noticed and remarked.' He was examining his fingers absently. 'Little whispers have come my way to the effect that we don't get on, that we disagree.' The lids lifted and there was a keener edge to the eye and voice. 'Before we know where we are rumours will be flying around that there's a rift in the management of *The Chequered Silence*. Such rumours have a way of escalating and we don't want that to happen, do we?' and he tilted a brow at her, regarding her intently.

Leah held his look for a few seconds and then averted her eyes, furiously evaluating his words. It was so humid she could hardly think clearly and there was the beginnings of a dull, persistent pain in her temple that promised a splendid headache. She brought her eyes back to his, aware that he had been watching her steadily all this time, and said carefully:

'It's been a long day. Max, what's the point of all this?'

'I don't like mysteries.'

'I'm tired and hot and I want to go home. Max, drop it, please.'

'Sorry. I'm a tenacious devil.'

'You weren't very tenacious five years ago.' The words were out even before Leah realised they were lurking in her head and she stared at him, aghast. There was a moment of incredulous silence, then Max's hand shot out and pulled her round to face him.

'Like hell I wasn't,' he said softly, anger banked down ominously. 'I very nearly squeezed your agent's neck trying to get information from her—did she tell you that? I haunted the places where we used to meet, scanned the theatre pages for news of you. Short of putting a detective agency on to your trail there wasn't a lot more I could do—and I even thought of doing just that, but you'd made it very plain you didn't want to see me again.' He shook her. 'Do you mean to tell me that you were waiting for me to find you?' The words were snapped out and Leah, white-faced, blurted out:

'No! No, of course not!' but was struck by the daunting thought that there might be some truth in the accusation. *Had* she expected him to search her out? Deep down, subconsciously, had she been waiting for him to find her? It was a shattering thought and sent the blood rushing to her cheeks, and she said again: 'No.'

'Well, that's something, because believe me, lady, the brush-off was eloquent enough.' He paused, brown eyes glittering down at her, and added significantly: 'So I thought then. Now, I'm not so sure.'

Through stiff lips, Leah protested huskily: 'Max, you're hurting me!'

Her wrist was flung down and hands gripped her upper arms as he exploded:

'Does that surprise you? My God! I'm not a violent man, but you do have the happy knack of lighting the fuse. I thought our past was decently buried, but . . .' He pulled her into his arms and kissed her. It started out savage but soon changed, seducing all the latent, banked-down feelings that had lain dormant for so long, evoking old longings, remembered ecstasies. When their lips at last parted, Max said harshly: 'Now we're coming to the crux of the matter, aren't we? I don't think I'm God's gift to any woman, Leah, but I sure as hell know when a relationship is on the way out. A cooling off in no way described what we had together. I had difficulty believing it then and I find it incredible to believe now.' His hand raked through her hair, cupping the back of her head, holding her still, the other hand curving round her back, folding her to him. 'There was never anything cool about us, Leah, was there? Even after five years, it's still the same.'

Her whole being in tumult, breathing uneven, limbs trembling so much that Max was supporting her weight, Leah could not meet his eyes and closed her own, while his lips touched her lids, brushing lightly down her cheek, resting in the hollow of neck and shoulder.

'All these weeks you've been fighting me, haven't you?' His mouth found hers again, sweetly tantalising. 'Fighting yourself,' he accused, his voice coaxingly velvet soft.

It was all true—all of it. Leah lay in his arms, knowing that from the very first moment he had walked into the angels' reception it had been inevitable that this should happen.

'Haven't you?' Max gave her a gentle shake, his voice low and demanding. He kissed her again, then moved his hand from her hair and caught up her wrist, his fingers resting gently on the pulse, saying: 'Can't you feel the blood coursing through your veins? Feel your heart racing? Feel mine?' and he placed her unresisting hand across his chest, palm down against the steady pounding of his heart, before resting his own upon her breast, tenderly and oh! so sweetly familiar.

Leah buried her face in his shoulder, feeling the beating of his heart beneath her hand, exulting in the strength of his body, the warmth of his hand, the smell, the feel of him, even down to the roughness of his jaw against her cheek. His hand came up to lift her face. He asked: 'Can you look me in the eyes and honestly say that Eliot Yates is the man for you?'

She froze—and asked quietly: 'Is this the point of the exercise, Max?'

His face wiped clean of any expression, he looked at her, and replied evenly: 'Would it be so bad a thing if I said yes?'

Leah placed her hands against his chest, and at the first hint of pressure he released her and she backed away two paces. They contemplated each other, Max curiously still, Leah, her breathing shallow and her emotions screaming to a halt, as footsteps came clattering up the stairs and the door swung open. Michael exploded into the room and walked briskly towards them, bristling with energy and normality, unaware of the vortex into which he now halted.

He said: 'Thought I'd catch you both still here. Well?' He looked first to Leah and then to Max, whom he asked: 'What does Leah think?'

Max said: 'I haven't had time, Michael, to discuss it with her yet.'

'Oh. Well, no time like the present,' and Michael dragged a chair over and seated himself, gesturing for them to do likewise.

All feelings suspended, and wearing a well-schooled mask, Leah asked: 'Discuss what?'

'You tell her, Max,' ordered Michael, 'it's your idea, after all,' and he sat back, arms folded.

Max drew a chair forward for Leah and after a slight hesitation she seated herself. For some reason she suspected that Max was reluctant to divulge this idea while Michael was present, but was having his hand forced. He moved a chair for his own use but did not sit, instead he leaned, arms straight, hands grasping the wooden backrest. He began to speak slowly, voice devoid of expression.

'You know from experience, Leah, that where a new play is concerned it is often the practice to alter during rehearsal and an element of workshop is involved in the direction. You also know that in any production there are benefits from a joining together of ideas and feelings between director, actors and where possible, playwright. Ever since I first read *The Chequered Silence* I haven't been totally satisfied with the ending.' He held up his hand as Leah made to speak. 'Please—hear me out.' He thought for a moment, then continued: 'Reading it, my dissatisfaction was a nebulous thing, an instinctive, indecisive unease which I initially thrust to the back of my mind, where it lay dormant but still viable. This uneasiness about the ending returned during early rehearsals, but again I chose to ignore it, knowing that the gradual building up of character and plot would resolve it, one way or the other. We've now reached the stage when I'm of the opinion that the final pages of the play need to be re-written.' He inclined his head towards her and waited, his face showing courteous interest.

Leah glanced at Michael, who was not even looking at them, but at his feet, chin sunk on chest. She returned a level gaze at Max, and said: 'I see,' and then, more strongly, a touch of sarcasm underlying the question: 'And what does our playwright have to say about this—nebulous, instinctive uneasiness of yours?'

Michael made a slight movement but did not speak. Max said:

'Naturally, as soon as I was sure in my own mind, I discussed my feelings with Eliot . . .'

'You didn't think, perhaps, that you should have broached the subject with me first?' How the question came out so cool, Leah could not imagine, for inside she was boiling.

'I would have discussed it with you both, together, had that been possible, but you've been out of town and I didn't feel I could hold the production back any longer, time is running out. I did speak briefly with Michael, just to keep him informed of what might happen, but really, nothing much could be talked over until I sounded out Eliot's views.'

'And of course, Eliot agreed with you entirely.' The sarcasm was clearly marked now and Leah could feel two spots of angry colour on her cheeks. She was aware of Michael, taking a definite back seat, watching them both carefully, and she found she was resenting deeply the brilliant control in the tall figure standing by the chair.

'No, I wouldn't say that,' Max was saying impartially. 'It must be exceedingly hard when you've given birth to a play to have any part of it challenged, and the ending especially so, but there was enough in what I felt for Eliot to overcome his initial rejection and to say he'd think about it. He went away and did so. Then he sat down and rewrote another ending on the lines I'd discussed with him.'

She held his look, stating flatly: 'I saw Eliot this afternoon. He didn't say anything of this.'

For the first time, Max hesitated in his reply, giving his words some consideration before speaking. 'Perhaps he was unsure of your reaction. He thought it would be better that I talk to you, after rehearsal today. Which is what I intended. Michael merely jumped the gun slightly.'

Sick with miserable anger, directed at herself and everyone else, Leah prompted: 'You're telling me that it's all cut and dried.'

Max gave a negative movement, observing firmly: 'By no means. We're awaiting your own views on the rewrite. Only the last three pages have been altered. You can read them for yourself in a moment, but basically, what we're doing is to change a straightforward conventional "happy ending" into an open one, one deliberately ambiguous, one the audience can choose for itself.'

'Isn't a happy ending in fashion this year?' asked Leah, raising scathing brows. 'Don't you believe in happy endings?'

The measured look, a slight tightening of the jaw were followed by calm patience. 'What I believe is immaterial, Leah, you know that. What we're looking for here is an ending theatrically acceptable. The one we have now is too smooth, too bland, not in keeping with the rest of the play, which asks awkward questions and pokes a finger at society in general and stirs up a number of issues that need qualifying.' He leaned forward, picking up some typed papers stapled together that were lying on the table. 'I realise it will be almost as difficult for you to accept the change as it was for Eliot. The play has been obsessively part of you for a long time.' He held out the sheets to her. 'Will you read it now, with as unbiased a mind as you can achieve? It won't take you long.'

Unhurriedly Leah rose to her feet, her eyes first on the manuscript, lifting to Max's face. She took it, saying: 'And if I don't agree?'

He regarded her thoughtfully. 'We'll cross that bridge if, and when, we have to. Remember, Leah, we're looking for a theatrically acceptable ending.'

Leah gave a sweeping side glance to Michael, whose face told her nothing of his own opinion on the subject, before walking to the other side of the room, halting at the window where she rested the manuscript on the wide ledge. She smoothed back the hair from her face, which felt hot and sticky. She took a handkerchief from the side pocket of her dress and dabbed her brow and her palms, and only then, taking a deep breath, did she pick up the manuscript and begin to read.

She read it through twice to be sure, then walked back to the two men who were talking quietly together. They broke off their conversation when she joined them, looking at her expectantly— Michael's grey eyes bright and alert in curious contrast to Max's, hooded lids secretive and dark depths dull and almost indifferent.

Leah was thinking how ironic life was—how diabolically ironic! Always good for a laugh, was life.

She stood, weighing the pages in her hand as she

said reflectively: 'I should have to see it in rehearsal before I was totally sure, but I think you're probably right.' The inward irony deepened when she saw a flicker of some expression, she couldn't tell exactly, that went through the indifferent brown eyes. Michael's grey ones were warm with approval and he was grinning complacently, saying:

'Nothing stiff-necked about Leah Durrance!'

She smiled faintly, although there was little warmth in her eyes. She asked Michael: 'Is your opinion the same?'

'Yes, it is. I wouldn't have picked it up myself, mind, but now it's been pointed out to me, I can see what Max means. This way there's a sting in the tail as well as in the body.' He thrust his chair under the table. 'I'm off. I'd also like to see the run-through of the new piece when it's ready.' He began to walk to the door, then stopped, slapping his thigh impatiently. 'Damn! Nearly forgot to give you a message, Max.' He swung round. 'Stephanie Farrel phoned through to the office to say she's picking you up from here instead of from the flat.' He smiled at them both. 'When's the interview with Miss Farrel coming off, Leah?'

She said: 'Next week.'

'Excellent. Well—goodnight to you, both,' and with a brisk salute of the hand, Michael was through the door and clattering down the stairs, the bang of the outer door sounding hollowly loud up the stairwell.

Max said, at last: 'I didn't think you'd agree. I misjudged you. I apologise.' A brow quirked. 'But only on that score. For nothing else.'

Do not, he was saying, include what has gone before—I still stand by the accusations, the bruises now forming on the flesh of your wrists and the kisses . . . especially the kisses.

The apology, taken at face value, was accepted by another meagre smile and a slight movement of her head. Her spirit had taken such a knock during the past hour that anything further merely touched on the periphery of her emotions. Her allegiance was not to the girl who had lain trembling in his arms but to the cool, self-assured woman whose head was held high, a little pale, perhaps, but composed. The madness had gone, the fever abated. She was down from Cloud Nine and landed firmly on two feet again, but it would take time for the feelings to flow through her, for the pain to dull.

She said: 'Tell me, Max, putting aside theatrical endings, which one would you, personally, choose? Do you consider our lovers to have a chance together?'

'No,' responded Max, giving her a searching look. 'No, I don't. There's too much going against them.' There was no hesitation or prevarication in his reply and Leah nodded thoughtfully, as if this were the answer she had expected. Max added: 'And you?'

'I don't think they have a chance either.' She gave a faint, mocking smile. 'You didn't expect that, did you? You thought me a romantic escapist, but I'm not. I'm a realist, like yourself,' and you've just proved how right I was to leave you, she added silently to herself. She picked up the folder and case and gave a swift glance at her watch. 'I must go.' She walked to the door, and when she stopped and looked back Max was still regarding her, his face shuttered and inscrutable. She said over her shoulder, her hand already on the door: 'I look forward to seeing the new ending when I get back from Nottingham. Give my regards to Miss Farrel. Goodnight Max.'

She gained the street and saw, out of the corner of her eye, a car slide into the kerb, Stephanie at the wheel. Leah did not break her stride. There was nothing she wanted to say to Stephanie Farrel—except, perhaps, beware of inscrutable men, but the cool, elegant Miss Farrel could look after herself, Leah was sure.

She extravagantly hailed a taxi, thinking: What the hell, it's not every day one's proved right, even though the proof is unpalatable.

How blind can one be? she thought with resignation, leaning back against the seat, closing her eyes, suddenly exhausted by heat and emotion. *The Chequered Silence* had been an extension of herself and Max—with a happy ending, and Max had thrust reality into that too. And quite rightly. The play would be better for it.

The driver swung his cab into a convenient space outside Walsh Productions. Riding the lift, Leah wondered if they would ever give each other any peace. Would Max be satisfied now that he had proved that he still had a physical power over her?

A laugh escaped her lips as she stepped into her office. She was thinking that peace, like happy endings, only came to a deserving few.

CHAPTER SEVEN

'I DON'T see why it has to be changed,' said Ann. 'I think the ending is just right as it is.' She set the mug of coffee on to the small table by Leah's armchair and crossed to the sofa, curling herself into a corner, taking care not to spill her own coffee.

'That's because you're a romantic,' commented Leah, lifting her head from the book she was trying, not too successfully, to read. Since leaving Max she had hardly had one coherent thought in her head, and the book was supposed to divert her agile mind away from questions and conjectures that she was unable to satisfy. Even Ann now seemed to be a stranger, to be regarded through new eyes, after Max's assertion that she was in love with Eliot.

Small, rounded, with a puckish charm, Ann King protested mildly: 'I don't think I'm a romantic. I know quite a few couples in similar circumstances to the couple in the play who've married and are living happily and successfully together.' She paused and gave a gamin scowl. 'And I shall tell Eliot so.'

'Don't go confusing real life with the theatre,' Leah said dryly and Ann replied quickly:

'Hah! I thought that was what the theatre was supposed to depict!' and grinned cockily.

'Only the slice of life we want it to show—in other words, we're in control. In life we have very little.'

'Well, you tell me how a happy ending weakens the play,' went on Ann stubbornly.

'I suppose it's because real life doesn't always consist of a happy ending, it's mostly compromise,' Leah suggested, speaking slowly, working out how best she could explain her feelings. 'Look—in the play John, a hearing man, and Elizabeth, a deaf girl, fall in love and we follow their lives, see them facing the problems that arise, both socially and emotionally, and true to life, it's not roses, roses all the way. Near the end they meet with a major crisis which is resolved by their love for each other overcoming everything else.' She paused for a drink of coffee. 'Curtain comes down. Audience claps and goes home. They've learnt something of being deaf in a society geared for the hearing. It will have made an impact on some, reaffirmation for others. Now—the new ending differs only in as much as there is no definite conclusion. The same major crisis is reached but is not totally resolved, leaving an equivocal ending, the audience choosing its own solution. Curtain comes down. Audience claps and goes home and says—how do you think things develop? What do you think happens? We leave them with a talking point. The romantics can opt for everything coming up roses, the realists, or shall we say, the sceptics, probably reject the happy ending syndrome. The only people we won't satisfy are those who can't make up their own minds and like the playwright to do it for them.'

Ann gave a chuckle at that before pulling a rueful grimace. 'Yes, I can see what you're getting at. I'm too hopelessly involved with Elizabeth, that's my problem. I need to believe in the happy ending. I feel as though I'm being rejected along with her.'

'Elizabeth isn't being rejected,' argued Leah. 'She's standing on her own two feet demanding that she be treated as a whole person in her own right.'

'I shall still tell Eliot what I think of his lousy new ending,' Ann promised darkly, and Leah, smiling, said:

'You do that,' and returned to the book, although she gave up reading after a few minutes. Ann and Eliot. Could there be some truth in what Max claimed? She felt, somehow, that there was. Max had a keen ear and eye . . . and had been in their company for long periods these past weeks. What he need never know was the relief she felt! Deep down she had known she could never marry Eliot, but it had taken Max coming back into her life to show her. She would make Eliot understand, in the kindest possible way, that there was no future for them together, then Eliot might look at Ann with different eyes. She thought back to when she had first met them, at the Deaf Mission, and tried to remember whether she had sensed anything but friendship between them, and could not. She had been involved in her own private anguish at the time and would not have noticed. Poor Ann, defending her happy ending!

Leah's gaze rested thoughtfully on her friend. She disapproved of matchmaking, having been subjected to it herself by well-meaning friends, but a gentle nudge at Cupid's arrow was permissible. It was up to Cupid to do the rest.

Coming to such a decision, she fetched pen and paper and wrote a short note, enclosing the two tickets for a concert at the Barbican that she had found waiting for her at the office that evening. As she addressed the envelope she hoped that Eliot would have the sense to ask Ann to go with him. Licking the flap, she said:

'Ann, can you give this to Eliot for me tomorrow, please? You'll be seeing him, won't you?'

Ann looked up from reading the evening paper. 'If they're going to work on the new ending he's sure to be there,' she agreed, reaching for the envelope and slipping it inside her bag. 'Goodness! I've only realised now that this means Oliver will have extra sign language to learn. Poor old Oliver! He's worked so hard, hasn't he? And have you seen Max lately? He's getting quite proficient.' She hesitated and looked at Leah uncertainly. 'You never use hand-sign at rehearsal, Leah,' and there was a slight rise in inflection almost making it a question.

'I don't need to, do I?' prevaricated Leah. 'I suppose, at first, I didn't want to outshine Oliver. I thought it better for him to only look a fool in front of his teacher—you know how complicated it is, at the beginning.' She gave a shrug. 'Once I'd not let on it was difficult—no, not difficult, unnecessary, to own up.'

'Maybe, but he knows.'

'Oliver does?'

Ann nodded. 'I think Nancy let it slip. No one else does, I'm sure. It doesn't matter, does it?'

'Not in the least,' replied Leah lightly.

Ann folded the paper and stretched her arms. 'It's rather sweet how everyone has learned some basic signs, isn't it? The good-mornings, the hellos and the how are yous. Nancy is awfully touched that they've bothered.'

'They're a friendly company,' agreed Leah, adding with some asperity: 'And yet why not? If

Nancy had been a foreigner they would surely have made some attempt to communicate with her. Don't be so bloody humble, Ann!' She stopped, frowned and put aside her book, moving swiftly to sit herself down by her friend, giving her a hug. 'I'm sorry. It's easy for me to talk, isn't it? but it makes me so mad, other people's attitude. It offends me to hear you being grateful. Rather like the crumbs from the rich man's table.'

Ann chuckled, her eyes resting with warmth and affection on the other girl. 'I owe you a lot,' she remarked, and startled, Leah retorted:

'Don't be such a wet!'

'It's true,' Ann went on, ignoring her friend's snort of derision. 'When you invited me to share this flat with you I walked on air for days. We deaf people are difficult to live with. We can be exasperating at times, the more so because we can't help it. Oh, I know I have partial hearing, and that's a tremendous advantage over total deafness, but the fact remains that I have a disability and you chose to live with me, knowing that.'

'My dear Ann, I never give your hearing a thought,' protested Leah, distressed.

'Maybe not consciously, but you do, without realising it,' said Ann, smiling. 'You always speak to me, face to face, did you not realise? And you speak clearly and don't shout, not like some people who think volume is what's required rather than clarity. Then I have to thank you for giving me Nancy's understudy . . .'

'I'm not staying to listen to you any more,' Leah scolded, rising quickly to her feet. 'I'm going to pack, and then I shall go to bed, I've an early start tomorrow.' She glared down at her friend. 'And let's have less of this nauseating gratitude and mousy modesty! You were given the understudy because, after Nancy, you were right for the part, and I invited you to share the flat because you like housework and can cook better than me!' and on that note she departed, the sound of Ann's laughter in her ears.

She managed to forget about Eliot while she was in Nottingham and waited until her return before broaching the subject of their future relationship. It was rather tricky, as Eliot had never actually asked her to marry him; she had always managed to steer him clear of popping the question. In the end she decided on the direct approach, couched in careful phrases, and after going quiet for a moment, Eliot said:

'Is it because of the re-write?'

Leah shook her head in denial. They were sitting in the Pineapple, a pub with a Victorian flavour in decor and architecture, and a popular midday haunt of the company of *The Chequered Silence* because of its close proximity to the rehearsal room. Its popularity today was no exception, and Leah could see her colleagues' faces dotted here and there among the locals. She and Eliot were somewhat isolated from the others and she had said her piece, hoping to shield them both from an emotional scene by their lack of privacy.

'No, Eliot,' she replied, 'it has nothing to do with that—how could it?'

She lifted her head to find Max's eyes upon her. He was too far away for her to read his expression, but she found her cheeks growing warm and shifted uncomfortably, dropping her gaze. Damn the man, he wasn't omniscient, he couldn't possibly know what she was doing! she thought defensively.

'How could it?' she repeated, and Eliot shrugged. He took a drink of his beer, staring moodily into the contents. A plate of sandwiches, placed between them, was hardly touched.

'I don't know. Perhaps you think I shouldn't have changed it?' he suggested, and she replied patiently:

'If I'd thought that, I'd have fought tooth and nail, you know that, Eliot. Surely this morning's rehearsal has convinced you, if you needed convincing, that the re-write is a much stronger ending?'

He nodded, his eyes searching her face. 'I know I've no right to ask,' he said diffidently, 'but is there someone else, Leah?'

She glanced towards the bar. Max was still looking their way, rather absently, listening to Oliver and Charles, who seemed to be having a mild argument.

'Oliver?'

Her head came round with a jerk and she said incredulously: 'Oliver? Eliot, I've known Oliver for years, we were in training together, but we're nothing more than good friends.' She knitted her brow and said: 'Look, Eliot, there is someone—from way back, but it's all rather complicated. I thought I could forget him, but I find I can't. I'm sorry—I did try, Eliot, but it's no good.' She bit her lip and looked at him anxiously. 'I'd be sorry to lose your friendship. You're very important to me.'

'But not important enough.' Eliot downed the rest of his drink and stood up. 'Don't look so upset, Leah. I've half suspected this would happen, and we'll keep in touch.' He gave a good attempt at a smile. 'I hope everything works out well for you.'

Leah watched him join the others at the bar and there followed a general exodus of company people, leaving Max. He walked slowly over, glass in hand, and said: 'May I?' indicating Eliot's vacated chair, and she said: 'Of course,' and with his usual indolent grace Max seated himself. He eyed the sandwiches, observing:

'You don't seem to have much of an appetite, either of you.'

'Too hot,' Leah replied briefly.

Studying his highly polished, handmade shoe, Max went on casually: 'I was surprised to see Ann and Eliot at the Von Karajan concert the other evening.'

Leah arched her fine brows. 'Were you? They're both keen on orchestral music. Ann mentioned that she'd seen you. Did Miss Farrel enjoy the programme?'

'I believe so.' He lifted speculative eyes to hers.

'I'm rather fond of Mussorgsky and Ravel, for that matter, myself. Was the Berlin Philharmonic in good form?'

'I thought so, yes.'

Leah continued to hold his stare, her face showing only mild interest. Where had those few moves taken them, on the chessboard? she idly wondered. Stalemate. She lifted her wrist and glanced at her watch. 'I think it's time we left. The taxi will be here in a moment.' She rose to her feet and allowed Max to pave a way for her through the still busy bar and they gained the street. She was very much aware of the incongruity of their apparel compared to the rest of the Pineapple patrons and wondered, with some amusement, what the comments would be as they departed. 'Ah, well, they're theatricals,' would be the obvious one.

Max was wearing a lightweight pale grey suit, a dark blue shirt and a white tie, and Leah thought that he only needed a white trilby and white patent shoes to look a perfect character out of an American gangster film.

She had purposely dressed with care that morning. They were on their way to attend the interview for the magazine *Woman's View*, and photographs were to be taken. She had chosen a favourite Jean Muir, the cream background with red patterning was cool and comfortable as well as being smart, and there was a hint of the nineteen-thirties in the style that appealed to her. This interview was not one she was particularly looking forward to, and Leah felt she needed all the help she could get.

There had been a nice feeling of togetherness that morning when they had both turned up for rehearsal already dressed for the interview, and they had received teasing comments from the company in full force. Then, the frivolity over, they had begun a tough rehearsal, going over and over the new ending until Max was satisfied.

Like most things apprehensively approached, the meeting at the magazine's offices was not as difficult as Leah had imagined. The interview was conducted by one of Stephanie Farrel's minions, and Leah deliberately steered her answers away from the two-year professional blank in her life. Max, causing more than one heart to beat more quickly as he walked through to the interview room, was at ease and fluent, asserting that having a woman producer made little difference in his job, the accent being on the job itself, rather than the sex of his colleague. He wanted it to go on record that the producer and director of *The Chequered Silence* were in total accord and worked in perfect and close harmony. He had shot Leah a wicked side glance on saying this, and she wondered what interpretation Stephanie Farrel would put on that little bombshell of a statement.

Towards the end of the interview Stephanie joined them, and Leah was glad of the Jean Muir, for the editor was a picture of sophistication in pale lilac and impeccably groomed. While Max was in conversation with the photographer, Stephanie drew Leah to one side, saying:

'Max doesn't talk a great deal about the play. Is it going well?'

'I'd say we've reached the stage in rehearsal that can be expected at this date,' Leah replied cautiously, adding: 'I'm afraid we theatricals are wary of tempting the gods.'

Stephanie smiled. 'I'm longing to see it. First nights are such exciting affairs, aren't they?' She hesitated, her eyes going momentarily to Max, before returning to Leah. 'I'm giving a small dinner party on the tenth, I suppose you could call it a housewarming, although it's a little late, I've been in some weeks. Do say you'll come?'

'It's very kind of you, but I'm afraid the tenth is impossible,' Leah said pleasantly. She had no idea whether the date in her diary was free or not, but she had no intention of accepting. That kind of self-inflicted punishment she could do without.

'What a pity. Perhaps another time?' Stephanie answered, with just the right amount of regret in her voice, then excused herself. She approached

Max, who turned and smiled down at her, giving her his full attention. Now why on earth did she ask me? wondered Leah, watching the dark head bend closer to the fair one, and as she and Max left the building, inwardly digested the fact that Stephanie was not now living with Max, as she supposed, at Eaton Square. This piece of information was certainly interesting, and Leah quickly squashed an inner voice that mockingly enquired: only *interesting*?

Standing in the sunshine, Max looked at his watch. 'It's four o'clock. Too late to do any good at rehearsal.' He gave her a tilting glance. 'We're close to a gallery where a friend of mine is having an exhibition of his paintings. I have tickets for the private viewing, which is today. If I'm playing hookey I might as well have my producer along with me, as a partner in crime, if she cares to join me?'

Leah opened her mouth to automatically refuse, then thought, why not? She replied: 'Most sensible of you. Thank you, I should like to come with you.'

It was an interesting exhibition and the afternoon unwound like a brightly coloured canvas. Walking round the gallery with Max, a sherry in her hand, Leah felt a lightness of spirit that was hard to explain. Max, too, seemed to have shed some of his former reserve and was in excellent form. Perhaps they were both acting out a scene with characters that had no past and no future, only the present? she pondered whimsically.

She was introduced to the artist and to the gallery owner and to innumerable people who greeted Max warmly and eyed her with thinly veiled speculation. Max bought a small water-colour of a barge on a canal, and they watched the Sold sticker going up before they took their leave.

'Remembering the dismal sandwiches at the Pineapple, I suggest we eat,' said Max. 'How does that sound?'

'Like an excellent idea,' laughed Leah, suddenly aware of a gaping hole in her stomach.

'Good. Somewhere fairly close.' Max frowned in thought. 'If I take you to Napoleon's would it spoil the day?' he asked, a dark brow raised in question, the brown eyes suddenly blank.

Holding his look, Leah suggested lightly: 'Shall we find out?' and without further comment Max turned in that direction, his fingers politely cupping her elbow as they crossed the busy street.

'Monsieur Calvert! *Comment ça va?*' Monsieur Langeais came hurrying forward, a smile on his lips, bald dome shining in the soft pink light of his restaurant. His eyes moved on to take in Leah and his smile broadened, his moustache displayed to its fullest effect, his voice deepening. 'Ah, *mademoiselle!*' His glance to her left hand was brief but competent. '*Mademoiselle, bonsoir* ... it is a pleasure to see you once more,' and he imperiously gestured to a waiter, who escorted them to a window table and produced the menu.

'I promise you, Madame Langeais is still an excellent cook,' Max told her, his eyes on the choice of food. Leah looked round, her gaze sliding over their usual table, set in a far corner and secluded by bamboo and trailing plants. It was vacant. Too early for lovers, she thought wistfully.

The *patron* approached and launched into a tirade of French with Max who, in a suspended

pause, asked Leah: 'Are you willing to place
yourself in Monsieur's hands, Leah?' and when she
murmured her agreement, Monsieur Langeais
beamed his approval and walked to the kitchens.

Leah watched him go, then turned to Max,
saying delightedly: 'I can hardly believe it! The
place hasn't changed one little bit.' She smiled.
'Well, perhaps Monsieur has gained a few pounds
and lost a few hairs.'

'We're all older, and I trust, wiser,' remarked
Max enigmatically, signalling for the wine list.
Talk flowed easily through avocado, delicious
trout with mushroom stuffing, and came to a
slightly embarrassing halt on the arrival of
Monsieur Langeais himself carrying the sweet
course which he placed on the centre of the
table. Leah gave a quick up-sweep of her lashes
to find out Max's reaction to the heart-shaped
sweet and accompanying fresh strawberries. He
was saying:

'And what *spécialité* do you have for us here,
Monsieur Langeais?' and the *patron* replied with
due modesty: '*Coeurs à la crème*. I remember that
Mademoiselle has a partiality for the unusual,' and
he expertly scooped one of the heart-shaped
moulds on to her plate, to be followed by the
heart-shaped china dish filled with the strawberries.
He waited until Leah had tasted the sweet and
made the appropriate complimentary remarks,
then left them. Max drawled:

'Monsieur Langeais is a romantic optimist—a
devastating combination.'

'What part of France does he come from, do
you know?' asked Leah, refusing to be drawn.

'Tours, I believe.'

'Until I read your biography for the programme

notes I didn't realise that you were born in Scarborough.'

Contemplating the cheeseboard, Max made his choice and answered: 'It wasn't planned that way. Scarborough is the home of my maternal grandparents and my mother was visiting them at the time. I was impatient to be born and arrived on the scene early. My grandmother is still alive and extremely active. I see her when I can.'

'You really do have one foot in each country, don't you?' observed Leah enviously. 'You must have lots of relations here and in America.'

'Too many, sometimes.'

'Sooner too many, than too few,' argued Leah. She hesitated and went on diffidently: 'How are your parents? Your mother . . . your stepfather? I hope they're keeping well.'

Max seemed to take his time before answering, and when he did, his voice was even and unhurried. 'My mother is reasonably well. My stepfather died. It was expected, of course, but not, perhaps, quite so suddenly. I was able to see him before he died, which was something I'm grateful for. I flew over to be with him, if you remember.'

The waiter came with coffee and by the time it was poured Leah had some measure of control over her voice, but her face felt drained of all colour and the light had gone from the day. Stricken, she said:

'Max, I *am* sorry. I didn't know.'

He said easily: 'Don't look so distressed. It wasn't your fault that the timing was so bad. I'll admit I could have done with you being there, when I returned, but you weren't and that's that.'

He paused. 'I did phone you from the States, but I couldn't get through.'

'No. I wasn't answering,' she replied, without thinking.

'I also sent a cable, but you were not opening mail, either, were you?' he prompted casually.

'No.' She was thinking how cruel fate could be, and she the innocent means. How awful that Joss Calvert had died and Max had returned to England, expecting to be comforted by her, to find her gone and only that wretched letter to greet him! She looked up, frowned, and said: 'I'm sorry—what did you say?'

'Merely that Mrs Green, who I'm sure you remember was my weekly cleaning lady, was most concerned. You wouldn't let her in to do her work.' The brown eyes were guileless. 'You told her you had 'flu.'

'Oh. Yes, that's right.' Did I say that? I can't remember, thought Leah. All that period is a muddled haze. To her relief Max changed the subject and by the time they left Napoleon's her spirits had again lifted, due entirely to Max's perseverance. She refused to wonder why he was making this effort—she would think about that later. In an unguarded moment she remembered Una Bell's outrageous statement that Max would try to get her into his bed, but the idea was banished as quickly as it came. This new-found camaraderie was too precious to destroy with bizarre speculations. It was enough to be charmed into lightheartedness, and dark thoughts could go to the devil!

'What are we going to do for the rest of the evening?' Max enquired, after the bill was paid and adieux given. The cooler night air greeted them, coupled with that special ambiance of people moving towards entertainment and pleasures rather than work and toil. 'It so happens,' he went on smoothly, 'that I have tickets for *Guys and Dolls* at the Olivier. Shall we avail ourselves of them?'

His poker-faced delivery was too much for Leah and she burst out laughing.

'Shall we? Are you joking?' she demanded. 'Those tickets are like gold! What are we waiting for?'

Max grinned, raising a hand for a taxi, and Leah said quickly:

'Do you mind if we stop off at the office first? I believe I shall need my jacket for later on.'

Once settled inside the cab, the address given, he said: 'While you do that, I'll collect my car. I'll meet you outside the office in fifteen minutes.'

A skeleton staff greeted Leah at Walsh Productions. She checked the memo pad, glad that there was nothing of importance that needed her immediate attention, and set about freshening up. She gave her face a quick once-over, brushed her hair and applied a liberal dash of perfume. She eyed the bright-eyed and flushed image in the mirror, thinking—this is only for today ... business back as usual tomorrow, I promise.

Max's white Porsche slid into the kerb and this time it was Leah who was waiting, early, slipping into the passenger seat quickly because of the pile-up of traffic. They did not talk as they negotiated the river crossing, but as they waited their turn for the car park he moved his head to look at her, breathed in deeply and drawled: 'Je Reviens. Very nice—very Leah.'

She blushed scarlet and gabbled foolishly: 'Yes, well, I do use other perfume.'

'Of course,' he concurred equably. 'It merely seems appropriate that you should be wearing this particular perfume this particular evening.'

Leah made no reply. Anything further would only send the whole conversation out of proportion.

The National Theatre was teaming with people. A string quartet was playing in the foyer and the bar and bookstall were doing a brisk trade. Leah turned sparkling eyes to Max, enthusing.

'Doesn't all this make you feel good?' she demanded, looking round her. 'This is what theatre is all about, isn't it? I don't mean the actual building—although the three-theatres-in-one complex is a marvellous idea—I've seen outstanding theatre in a tin hut! I mean the bringing together of people to share an experience. Someone once said, I can't remember who, that the audience is fifty per cent of the performance, and I don't think there's anything comparable to being part of that mass of feeling.'

'Unless it's sharing that feeling on the other side of the footlights,' offered Max, a wealth of meaning in his words.

She eyed him warily. 'I'm afraid that suggestion merely fills me with terror now,' and she smiled at someone over his shoulder and murmured the expected: 'Hello.'

Max turned his head, following her look, and nodded his own greeting, commenting dryly: 'The number of people we know here tonight is amazing.' He raised a quizzical brow. 'I trust you were not hoping to keep the event secret?'

'I wasn't, but perhaps you were?'

'Now why should you suppose that?' he asked,

guiding her up the stairs, following the signs to the Olivier Theatre, adding in amusement: 'And here's some more friends for the record.'

'Leah! Max!' Ruth turned to Michael, saying indignantly: 'You didn't tell me Leah and Max were coming tonight!'

Michael shrugged his shoulders and lifted his hands in resignation before explaining patiently to his wife: 'Possibly because I didn't know.' He gave his colleagues a grin. 'Coming to see someone else's success, eh?'

'How long has this been going on?' whispered Ruth darkly, and Leah murmured: 'Miss Farrel couldn't make it. I'm his last resort.'

They separated and made for their respective seats. Three hours later, with the songs of Frank Loesser ringing in her head, Leah lay back in the Porsche, supremely happy and exhilarated.

'I didn't think we British could produce a musical like the Americans,' she announced dreamily, 'but that show has made me change my mind.' Max gave her an amused side glance and returned his eyes to the front. She began to hum a tune from the show, breaking off to state unnecessarily: 'And *Guys and Dolls* is an American show, too.' She hummed some more. 'You know, when I saw you today,' she went on, 'I thought you looked like a character straight out of Damon Runyon. If Sky Masterson had broken his leg tonight, you could have gone on in his place.'

Max gave a deep-throated laugh. 'I doubt very much whether the rest of the audience would have agreed with you, once I'd opened my mouth to sing!'

Leah chuckled and soothed: 'You sing good in the shower,' then froze. God, what a thing to say!

Max replied without a pause: 'I can take it, then, that you've enjoyed tonight?'

Leah unwound in relief. 'I did. Thank you for bringing me, Max,' and he said: 'You're welcome.'

She frowned, her voice going serious. 'Makes me wonder about our play. I do hope we can pull it off. I'm not asking for a huge success ... just a little one will do.'

'Work is taboo, tonight,' ordered Max. 'Are you going to start giving me some directions to this apartment of yours or do I drive round Hyde Park all night?'

'Flat.'

'Flat what?'

'No, no ... flat, not apartment. You're in England now.'

'So I am. Very well, where is this flat of yours?'

As they climbed the stairs, Leah explained: 'No lifts, but it keeps Ann and myself fit. This area is mostly bed-sits or flats or private hotels. I like being so close to the Park, and Bayswater Road on a Sunday is fascinating—artists and craftsmen set out their wares along the Park railings. I have to shut my eyes—I'm a sucker for pictures.'

'Yes, I remember,' said Max.

'Ann is at Nancy's tonight,' Leah announced, inserting the key in the door. She half-opened it, then stopped. 'I didn't mean ... that is, I only ...'

'Wanted me to know that Ann is not in,' Max finished calmly.

'Yes.' Absurd to be so touchy. Even the most innocent of remarks were proving traitorous. She switched on a couple of table lamps and went to close the curtains. 'We have a balcony and often sit out in the summer. It's quite a climb, but I like being on the top floor. This is the main room,' she went on, looking round it critically, the greens and creams and the warm colour of rosewood furniture pleasing to the eye. 'Bedrooms and bathroom through there, and kitchen through here,' and she walked as she spoke and began to make coffee.

When she returned with the tray she urged: 'Do smoke, if you wish. There's an ashtray somewhere.'

'No, I won't sully this beautiful atmosphere. I rarely do these days. Only give in under extreme nervous debility.'

She pulled a sceptical face. 'You? Nervous? Never!'

'It pleases you, I believe, to consider me infallible,' he returned mildly. 'I assure you I have the normal human failings.'

Leah placed the tray on to a low table, knelt down on to the carpet and sat back on her heels, regarding him thoughtfully. 'No,' she said at last, 'I don't think you're infallible. You merely cover up better than most.' She picked up the coffee pot, murmuring: 'You don't take sugar, do you?' She hesitated, uncertain. 'Or have you changed?'

Max said slowly: 'No, I haven't changed.'

For some inexplicable reason the tempo was altered and the atmosphere charged with a new tension, as if the words they were exchanging were innocent and another language, unvoiced but understood by both, was underneath. Max was now looking down at a chessboard, studying the pieces which were set out in a half-finished game.

'You still play chess,' he stated. 'With Ann?'

'No. Ann doesn't play. That game is with Oliver.'

His eyes still on the pieces, Max observed: 'You're white?' He glanced at her briefly for her answer, and then: 'I fear your Knight is imperilled.'

'Yes, he is, isn't he? I am prepared, however, to lose him.' She held out his cup and he leaned forward to take it from her, saying:

'Perhaps you'd allow me to give you a game some time?'

Leah made a small motion with her head and took a sip of coffee. They both knew that he was already playing in a game with her and that he had very successfully taken her Knight. She was not, however, prepared to admit whether or not Eliot was important to her. Max was now moving round the room, studying the pictures on the wall. He stopped, eventually, at one in particular, which he gave special attention.

It was an oil painting, not a large one, showing an old building, still beautiful even in its decadence, a dark glimmer of water and the blurred shapes of two gondolas in the shadows. A memento of Venice. A gift given with laughter and kisses, left over from halcyon days of yester year.

Leah said quietly, a little defensively: 'It was mine, so I took it with me.'

'My dear Leah, of course you took it,' Max drawled. 'I was merely about to remark on the fact that you've kept it, that's all.'

'Of course I kept it,' she answered, stung. 'Was I to throw out everything that reminded me of you?'

'I don't know. You tell me.' He turned and studied her, eyes hooded, face austere.

'I might be keeping it because the artist could become famous one day,' she challenged.

Max inclined his head. 'As good a reason as any.'

She clattered her cup on the tray and stood up.

'But not the right one. I have a fondness for the time and the place.'

'I see.' He paused. 'That's reassuring. I thought you might have repudiated the memories as well as myself.'

Max left not long after. It was a bitter-sweet feeling. Today had been an exquisite interlude where the past had encroached only briefly. But the past was like the inexorable tide, it waited on no man. He had made no move to touch her and as she closed the door she could not decide whether to be glad or sorry.

Pressure of work built up and Leah seemed never to be off the telephone—arranging billing details, publicity announcements, writing personal letters to critics. She argued, cajoled and rushed round London, cleaving a path between the offices in Shaftesbury Avenue and the rehearsal room. It was good to be busy, for it gave her less time to think.

The opening date in Nottingham grew nearer. The technical crew travelled up first with the set and props, the actors following. On the Sunday there was a technical rehearsal in which lighting, sound and cue calls were ironed out and then on the Monday the play was given a good run through. Afterwards, Max called everyone on stage.

'There's nothing more I can do. It's all there, believe me, and you've shown me that we have the makings of a great production. All you need is those seats out their filled, and in a few hours you'll have that. Go now, get changed, have something to eat and try and rest.' He smiled. 'And good luck!'

The lights were blazing forth from the Theatre

Royal foyer, illuminating the pillared façade and the billboards, proclaiming '*The Chequered Silence*, a new play by Eliot Yates.'

A quiver of excitement shot through Leah as she approached and following the throng of people through the double doors and into the large foyer. She smiled a greeting to the Theatre Manager and made for her seat. She had been backstage to give her good wishes, seeing Max briefly. Eliot was already in his seat in the circle, sitting with Michael and Ruth. Stephanie Farrel was there, and the critics. The theatre was very nearly full, which, considering its large seating capacity, was encouraging.

When the curtain came down on the first act Leah mingled with the audience, hearing snatches of conversation, the play proving to be a talking point. On the final curtain Leah listened to the applause and felt lightheaded with relief. In her opinion the play had reached a peak in the acting never before reached in rehearsal, and even knowing it so well she was moved between tears and laughter, and she knew that she was not the only one.

She made her way backstage where Ruth rushed up, eyes shining, and they hugged each other, almost laughing and crying at the same time. Eliot looked dazed while Michael said simply: 'I think we're okay.'

Leah smiled shakily and replied: 'Let's wait for the reviews, eh?'

The critics agreed with Michael, and words like 'magical', 'riveting' and 'enthralling' were quoted and word-of-mouth praise shot round the region, filling the theatre throughout the week.

Michael gave a party on the final Saturday to which everyone involved in the production was invited. The party went with a swing, everyone letting down their hair before facing the real hard work that was to follow in New York. Leah found herself next to Max at one point in the evening, and she asked:

'How are you feeling about facing the Great White Way? The Street?' referring to the nicknames given to Broadway, and Max gave his slow smile, his eyebrows twisting comically.

'Broadway's a tricky number,' he admitted. 'More tricky than the West End, because it's substantially the home of comedy and musicals. We can fly in Nottingham and still bomb in New York quite easily.'

'Have another drink,' urged Leah wryly, and he laughed, adding:

'I'll confess to you that although I'm extremely guarded outwardly in my optimism, deep down I think this is a play which could make theatre history.'

'I'll drink to that,' said Leah, 'with my fingers crossed.' She drank. 'I don't mind admitting, I'm terrified!'

Heathrow Airport was its usual frenetic confluence. Leah paid off the taxi and wheeled her case into the terminal entrance. She made for the weighing counter and saw Max, leaning against a wall, luggage at his feet, reading a newspaper. He lifted his head as she went towards him and straightened, folding his paper.

'Max! What are you doing here?' she asked in amazement.

'Flying out with you.' He gave a faint smile. 'Does that upset you?'

Her colour deepening despite her poise, Leah said: 'No. Should it?'

'I hope not.' Max looked at the queue. 'Shall we line up?'

They weighed in and were given seats together, then made for the departure lounge.

'We've time for a drink. Coffee?' offered Max, and Leah smiled her agreement. It was too late to ignore that she was as much in love with Max now as she had been five years ago. All she could hope to retrieve from the debris was her dignity. Whether he had totally forgiven her for walking out on him or not, certainly the early hostility had disappeared, which made life easier. Easier, but not happier.

Happier? Who says happiness is a prerequisite to living? she asked herself scornfully. You be satisfied with what you've got, lady! What she had was a possible hit show on her hands and the promise of a satisfying career. She had made her mark and now she was on her way up. Once she had put *The Chequered Silence* safely on the road she could cut and run back home. Max would be staying; he was directing the American company. The Atlantic would be between them and perhaps she could pick up her life and get on with it.

She watched him waiting for the coffee at the counter and realised that she should have expected Max to go on ahead of the company. His family lived in America and there was nothing more he could do in London. The company was following in four days and then rehearsals would begin. During those four days Max would, apparently, be free to stay with his sister. Had her own invitation to visit Celia and Henry been instigated by Max, and not, as she had thought, by Michael?

She was frowning without being aware of the

fact. Stephanie Farrel had been much in evidence both at the first night and at Michael's party, and it had been necessary for Leah to be very gay and lighthearted, and Oliver, her old friend and nothing more, had assisted her, been her bulwark and prop. And now she was going to spend four days staying with Max's relatives and there would be no Oliver, no Eliot ... and no Stephanie.

'You're looking serious. Nervous of flying?' Max was standing before her. She took the coffee from him and grimaced a smile.

'Not really. I quite like take-off, but I'm not so keen on landing. It always hurts my ears—and yes, I've tried all the dodges, and nothing seems to do much good.'

'Some people seem to be more susceptible,' agreed Max, joining her on the bench. He glanced at the screen, checking their flight number. 'Never mind, I'll hold your hand. That might take your mind off things.' His glance came her way. There was no mockery in his voice or on his face and as each reply that came to her lips was instantly rejected, Leah gave none, and then their flight came up and they made their way to the departure gate.

No one can sit for nine hours on a plane without achieving a certain amount of intimacy with the next seat passenger, especially if the seats are two together by the window. Max took off his suit jacket—yet another one, a smart-looking grey flannel with a fine red stripe, beneath which he wore a deep burgundy striped shirt teamed with a grey tie. He folded it and placed it in the locker above the seats, then he took her own, an off-white linen, with it. The seat-belt signal began to flash and the plane taxied along the runway. When they had been in the air for some minutes, Max turned to her and said:

'Celia is looking forward to your visit,' and Leah replied:

'It's very kind of your sister to have me.'

'You didn't get to see much of New York, the last time you came over, I understand?'

'No. It was such an unexpected trip I hardly had time to catch my breath.'

'We'll have to see what we can do this time,' Max declared, and Leah murmured a reply and decided not to fight any more. Enough was enough, and she was only human. This man held her happiness in the hollow of his hand. The chess game was not fully played, but her defences were weakened and she didn't really care any more.

They ate, watched a film, ate again, and Leah slept, waking to find her head resting comfortably upon Max's shoulder. The pilot's voice came over the air, informing them that they were approaching John F. Kennedy International Airport and would touch down in half an hour. Leah craned to see out of the window, ready to catch sight of the impressive coastline. When her ears began to sting Max gave her a barley sugar, then her hand was firmly taken in his and she settled back and prepared to land, for the second time in her life, in the United States of America.

If someone had told her, that first time, that she would be coming again, and Max Calvert would be holding her hand, comforting her, she would not have believed them. It was difficult to believe, even now. yet there was his hand, slender and beautiful, clasping hers.

The wheels touched down. They had arrived.

CHAPTER EIGHT

'I'M so glad the play went well on its pre-run,' Celia said, preceding her into the bedroom. 'I'm longing for the first night, they're such exciting occasions. Henry says it's a sell-out already and that bookings are going extremely well for the run.' She looked round critically. 'I do hope you'll find the room comfortable.'

'I'm sure I shall,' responded Leah. 'It's kind of you to put me up at all.'

'I see so little of Max that I begrudge him going to a hotel,' confessed Celia. 'Henry's booked you both in at the St Regis on East 55th, Sunday onwards, but I wanted you and Max to rest up here first.'

You and Max? Leah looked at her sharply, but there was nothing to be read from Celia's open, friendly face.

'The bathroom's right opposite—the boys have been forbidden it, so it should stay decent,' Celia was saying with a grin, and Leah asked:

'How old are they?'

'Bobby's nearly eight and Chris is five. There's a washbasin in here, which is useful, and plenty of cupboard space—not that you appear to have brought much luggage with you.'

'And that door?' asked Leah, looking towards an interior door.

'That leads to what really is a dressing-room, but we use it as a spare bedroom.' Celia checked the handle. 'It's locked. Max is a quiet sleeper, although they made the walls good and thick in those days.'

'Does Max usually have this room when he comes?' asked Leah. 'Really, Celia, I'd much rather use the small room.'

'You wouldn't,' grinned Celia. 'I'll give you time to unpack. There'll be a drink on ice and something light to pick at, laid out in the dining room in half an hour. Shout if you want anything,' and with a smile, Celia left the room.

Leah sat down on the bed and eyed the door thoughtfully. Then she rose and went out of the room, walking the few yards down the landing and knocked on the first door, which should, by her reckoning, be the right one. After a few moments, Max answered the summons and opened it, in the act of pulling off his tie.

She said quickly: 'Max, I feel awful about taking your room. Won't you let me do a swop?'

He backed off and threw the tie across the back of a chair, beginning to unbutton his shirt. 'All I need is somewhere to sleep. Who's going to use the shower first?' The shirt was now off and a smooth brown back and then a broad, well-formed chest smudged dark with body hair was presented to her view.

'You can,' offered Leah, and fled.

Over the next three days she renewed her acquaintance with Celia and Henry Ross and knew that she could like them very much, if she allowed herself to. Max was obviously very fond of his sister and she was open in her affection for him.

Leah was given a desk in Henry's office, where she spent some of her time preparing for the arrival of the rest of the company, the remainder taken over with sightseeing—Max being her guide.

They began with a Circle Line boat trip round the Island of Manhattan, and sitting the furthest away from the official tour guide, an elderly ex-vaudeville artist who considered he was still doing his act, Leah was able to see the famous Manhattan skyline in all its glory, Max murmuring comments close to her ear.

As they passed the Statue of Liberty, he said: 'Did you know that this inspiring masterpiece, base and statue, stands three hundred and three feet, and was the work of Frederic Auguste Bartholdi, a gift of the people of France to the people of the United States?'

'Not until I read the guide book over your shoulder,' admitted Leah, laughing into his eyes, the wind whipping her hair across his face.

He took a fistful of hair and held her face close, and she caught her breath, waiting for the kiss ... which did not come. He smiled lazily, and drawled:

'Young women who mock might get thrown overboard.' He moved her into the shelter of his body, hands on the rails either side of her, continuing: 'Brooklyn, Manhattan and Williamsburg Bridges coming up,' his cheek close to hers as he spoke. 'There are the flags of the United Nations. An impressive sight, aren't they?'

Whatever game Max was playing, it certainly was not one he intended to hurry, thought Leah, feeling the warmth of his body against her as she leant on the rails, watching the passing sights. The Yankee Stadium, George Washington Bridge and the Little Red Lighthouse, Grant's Tomb, Riverside Park, were all pointed out along with other places of interest, and snippets of history given in that transatlantic drawl that had the power to send all sensible, coherent thought out of Leah's head.

'We've chosen a good day for the trip,' said Max, as they neared the end of their journey. 'We're about to pass the Ship Terminal and I believe the Q.E. 2 is docked—yes, there! do you see?'

'Isn't she beautiful?' said Leah, patriotic feelings stirring, and then, solemnly: 'Do you realise we've been on a thirty-five-mile boat trip and its taken us three hours?'

'Reading over your shoulder—yes,' said Max.

They returned, rosy-cheeked and laughing, and Celia made a good effort at hiding her smirk of satisfaction, but Leah caught it. If Max had, he gave no sign.

The second day they incorporated the World Trade Centre and a drive through Greenwich Village, ending up with dinner for two at the famous Plaza Hotel on Fifth Avenue, overlooking Central Park.

As Leah drifted to sleep that night she mused: I don't get this! Why hasn't he even kissed me yet? . . . Even?

The third day they took in the United Nations, the Rockefeller Centre where they lunched on the sixty-fifth floor in the Rainbow Room, Leah boggling at the panoramic view from the large glass windows, and finishing up at the Metropolitan Museum.

In the evening Celia gave a small dinner party. There was no redhead invited this time for Max. Leah was the bait.

She went into her bedroom later that evening with her emotions in a riot of confusion. All during the meal she had kept up a lively conversation with her immediate neighbours, but each time she glanced across the table she met Max's gaze, the sleepy effect of the hooded lids belied by the intelligent depths of the dark pupils. She glared at her reflection in the mirror and thought moodily that if this black number hadn't sent his pulse rate up, then nothing would! She stripped off and flung it on the bed, an action totally unwarranted, as the price tag would have proved, bra and panties following, then she opened a Bloomingdale's packet and withdrew with gentle delicacy a nightdress.

She slipped it on. She was tanned by now and the cream silk looked good against her skin. She stared for a long moment in the mirror, bottom lip caught pensively between her teeth as she eyed the low neckline, edged with lace, the thin straps and the shape of her body beneath the fall of the material.

Are you being reprehensible, Leah Durrance? she asked herself. Yes. Will you regret this, Leah Durrance? Probably.

She scowled at her image and turned away, approaching the washbasin—and stopped. And caught her breath in horror, staring, mesmerised. The held breath exploded out of her, followed by a convulsive shudder that shook her body.

Two enormous black, long-legged spiders were splayed out in a nightmare pattern, darkly etched against the pale blue porcelain.

'Oh, my God!' moaned Leah in deep revulsion, and backed away, coming up against the dividing door. Keeping her eyes locked on the washbasin, palms spread out against the wood, she called out urgently: 'Max! Max, are you there?'

There was a moment's pause, a movement, then his voice sounded close on the other side.

'Yes. What is it, Leah?'

'Can you c-come, please?' Her voice squeaked as she saw one of the brutes dart a couple of inches, and then, mercifully, stop.

'What's the matter?' and then, 'Leah, open the door. Leah! The key! It's your side.'

Still keeping her eyes fixed, she fumbled for the key and turned it. As it clicked, Max opened the door. As though glued to it, Leah backed up, and then she was in his arms.

His hands stroked her back comfortingly and Leah, her face buried in the warmth of his chest, thought, I don't care any more! I'm where I want to be.

'Good heavens, girl, what's the matter?' Max demanded, and after a moment, she gulped and replied quaveringly:

'There's t-two spiders in the ... b-basin, Max. Two!' and another shudder ran through her and he said quickly:

'It's all right, I'll deal with them. Wait here.'

'I don't want them killed.'

He smiled and said gently: 'I won't kill them.' He stayed for a second, an odd look on his face, then he gave her a little push into his room.

Leah sat down weakly on to a cane chair and took a couple of deep, steadying breaths. Two! Two great black, long-legged brutes!

In an amazingly short time Max returned, carrying a glass. She stood up. 'Where have you put them?' she asked anxiously.

'Outside, on the fire-escape.'

She gave a sigh of relief and pulled an apologetic smile. 'I'm sorry,' she murmured.

'Here, drink this. I thought you were going to faint.' Max handed her the glass and she tasted it tentatively.

'I only like brandy on Christmas pudding,' she told him, and he grinned.

'Don't worry, it won't get wasted. But have a sip, if you can. It will do you good.'

She did as she was told, then said indignantly: 'Have you ever seen such whoppers? H-how do you think they got there?' she added, her eyes downcast, contemplating the liquid in the glass.

'These are old buildings, you know, and have much in common with bookshops.'

Thick lashes lifted and Leah's green eyes widened in surprise; Max gave a slow smile, saying softly: 'You surely don't think I've forgotten how we first met?'

'I don't know—you could have.'

'Well, I haven't. And as for how they got there, they've probably come up the waste pipe. I've had a look round. There aren't any more.'

'I should hope not!' Leah gave another shudder. 'Can you positively guarantee that?' She eyed her room beyond Max and the open door with hostility. 'I'm going to be dreaming of spiders all night!' she vowed in disgust, and held out the glass. Max took it from her with one hand while claiming her hand with his other. Carefully he placed the glass on the tallboy and said:

'Would it help if *I* slept in that room tonight,' and gave her a whimsical look, 'and ward off any newcomers?'

Leah swallowed. Standing barefooted, she had forgotten how tall he was. The half undone evening shirt showed whiter than white against his tanned skin.

The scene is set, she thought; the actors are on stage and the director is working his own particular brand of charm and magic. Delightful, remembered sensations were passing through his hand to hers and the colour came slowly to her face.

'I think I shall still ... dream spiders,' she replied huskily, meeting his eyes.

Max lifted her hand and touched his lips briefly into the palm. 'Then perhaps I should give you something else to dream about?' he suggested. 'Mmm?' There was a smile in his eyes and a faint curve to his lips. When she did not, could not, speak, he took her other hand and held them both for a moment, bringing them to his lips, his eyes still holding hers.

'Have you stopped running, Leah?' he asked gently, and Leah gave out a long sigh and breathed: 'It seems I have,' and went into his arms, her lips meeting his in one fluid moment.

Some time during the night, her body warmed by his, she murmured:

'You remember Una Bell, my agent?'

'Do I remember Una Bell!' was the lazy reply.

'Una said, many weeks ago, that you would entice me back into your bed.'

There was a comfortable silence.

'And why did the redoubtable Mrs Bell say that?'

Leah stretched a cramped leg. 'To remind me of what I rejected.' She caught her breath as his hand, lying heavy against her hip, smoothed a sensitive path upwards to her face, gently turning it to his, lips touching briefly.

'She could be right,' Max drawled, and prepared to banish Una Bell from his bed forthwith.

The next morning, before breakfast, Leah cornered

cornered nearly-eight-year-old Bobby Ross and hissed indignantly:

'Why *two*, Bobby? I only paid you for one!'

The boy screwed up his freckly nose and replied virtuously:

'Uncle Max paid for the other.' His face cleared as he looked beyond her shoulder. 'It doesn't matter Leah knowing, Uncle Max, does it? It's not a secret from Leah?'

Leah swung round, agonised, to find Max leaning indolently against the doorway, amusement and enlightenment showing on his face, and something more . . . a hint of triumph, perhaps?

'No, Bobby, it doesn't matter Leah knowing,' he drawled, coming forward to ruffle his nephew's hair affectionately. The boy nodded, relieved, and hearing his mother call, ran to the door, stopped to turn and ask, puzzled:

'Why did you want the spiders, Uncle?'

Max turned a thoughtful expression to Leah. 'Why did we want the spiders, Leah?'

She glared at him. 'Well, you see, Bobby,' she began, floundering as she met the young boy's round-eyed gaze, 'your uncle and I, we . . .' She stopped, her brain refusing to work.

'Needed them for an experiment,' concluded Max.

'Oh.' Bobby thought that a perfectly reasonable explanation.

'We didn't kill them,' put in Leah quickly.

'Did it work?' enquired the formidable Bobby, and Max, his eyes on Leah who was refusing to meet his look, replied:

'I believe it did,' and Bobby said a cheerful: 'Good,' and darted out.

Leah waited until the door closed behind him

and with her face bright red, said weakly: 'I never was any good at conspiracy.'

'How much did you pay Bobby?' asked Max, his eyes amused.

'Two dollars,' Leah replied, allowing herself to be drawn against his chest. 'And you?'

'Four.'

'He obviously thought himself well paid.' Leah began to laugh softly, then lifting her head, she said: 'Max Calvert, you are a devious, scheming . . .' She stopped as his mouth swallowed her words.

Lifting his head, Max retaliated: 'Leah Durrance, you are a devious, scheming . . .' His words were stopped by Leah's hand across his lips, her eyes brimming with laughter. 'I admit I had a few uneasy qualms when I saw how upset you were,' he went on. 'I thought the wretched boy had merely been a little over-zealous, giving me two for the price of one!'

'I only asked for a teeny, tiny spider,' Leah mourned. She gave a shudder. 'Ugh! I wonder where he found them?'

'I can tell you exactly where he found them, only I don't think you're really interested.' Max paused and slanted her a glance. 'Thinking of running away again, Leah?'

She said: 'No.'

'Good. We'll have to talk. Shall we get the first night over and done with, mmm?' and relief, coupled with a ridiculous shyness, caused her to give a small nod of the head without speaking.

Two days later Leah walked into the theatre on 45th Street and thought how easy it had been to get back into a working relationship—Max as director and Max as lover were two different people. Just occasionally she would find his eyes upon her and a brow would be lifted or his lips would curve into a faint smile, and something intimate and precious would pass briefly between them, then she would carry on, her heart singing and happiness coursing wildly through her.

She had liked the John Golden Theatre from the very beginning, feeling it to be perfect for *The Chequered Silence*, and her first impressions had not changed. The technical rehearsal had gone well and tension and excitement were beginning to build up within the company for the opening night two days ahead. As she walked into the auditorium, Leah felt mild surprise that the rehearsal was not in progress. She understood that Max had called it for two o'clock, and peering at her watch in the semi-darkness she saw that it was nearer three. People were sitting or standing in groups around the stage area and there was an unmistakable air of despondency in their attitude and expression.

Leah stopped at the edge of the stage and asked abruptly: 'What's the matter?'

Oliver, standing with his hands in his pockets, staring down at his feet, lifted his head and said briefly: 'Everything,' and his voice was heavy with disappointment.

Anxiety made Leah glance round sharply, and when she saw that it was Henry leaning against the proscenium arch her eyes stopped on him and she asked curtly: 'Henry?'

He came forward slowly. 'I'm afraid the play will have to be cancelled, Leah.'

Bewildered, she asked: 'Why?'

As it was Charles on whom her incredulous questioning look rested, he answered: 'There's been an accident—Nancy and Ann. We're without an Elizabeth for opening night, and possibly for the rest of this week.'

'It might be worth while putting in a clause for the future that no leading actor travels with the understudy,' put in Henry gloomily, and Oliver flared:

'It was natural that they should be together. Nancy needs Ann. Without her she's totally cut off from people!'

Henry lifted a placatory hand, murmuring: 'Yes, I do understand, Oliver. This is an unusual case.'

'Will someone please tell me what's happened?' demanded Leah, her voice rising in frustration.

'We haven't got all the details, but it seems that Nancy wanted to visit the Empire State building during their break this morning and Ann and Eliot went with her. On the way back their taxi was in collision with two other vehicles, one of which was a bus,' Charles explained quietly. 'The news, so far, is that Ann has a suspected broken arm and that Nancy is unconscious.'

'And Eliot?'

'He's all right, apart from shock. He and the driver were unhurt—well, with any seriousness . . . all of them have cuts and bruises, from the impact and flying glass.'

His voice echoed in the empty theatre. Leah stared at him, trying to take in the enormity of what she had just been told. Her initial relief that no one had been killed was now being swamped by angry despair that such a thing should have happened to overthrow all their hopes and aspirations.

Henry said: 'Eliot telephoned Max, who went immediately to the hospital. They're now on their way back here.' He shrugged his shoulders philosophically. 'I can't foresee any hope, however. Ann can hardly go on and do sign language with a broken arm and Nancy is more than likely concussed, even if they don't find anything else the matter with her, which God forbid!'

There was a poignant silence and then, feeling her legs giving way, Leah sat down on the nearest front row seat. She gave a deep, therapeutic sigh and said matter-of-factly: 'Well—that's that.'

The silence lengthened as each digested Henry's words which had managed to sabotage any slight feelings of hope that had been flickering in spite of what common sense told them.

The rear doors opened and Max strode in, followed by Eliot. Leah turned in her seat and watched them come down the centre aisle. Max's face was calm and controlled, his eyes perhaps a trifle strained and his lips tighter than usual if one looked closely. Eliot, on the other hand, looked stricken, every line of his body despondent and unhappy. He had more reason, perhaps—as the plaster across his bruised and swollen forehead proclaimed. No one spoke until they reached the stage. Max's eyes swept over the whole company, not giving Leah any special attention, his mind working furiously with the problems on hand. Charles spoke for all of them, asking:

'How are they?'

Max said factually: 'Nancy has regained consciousness, nothing seriously wrong with her, apart from the blow to the head, but they're keeping her in for observation. She certainly won't be fit for Wednesday. Ann has a broken arm which has now been set. They're both suffering from shock.' He turned to Henry. 'We shall have to cancel, I'm afraid, Henry. Can we leave that to you?'

His brother-in-law's, 'Sure,' came out heavily.

'What a mess!' Eliot groaned, leaning against the stage and putting his head in his hands. 'It all happened so quickly.'

'I suppose we *have* to cancel?' Charles asked thoughtfully. 'The American actress won't be anywhere near ready to take over, I presume?' He directed his question at Henry, who shook his head.

'I very much doubt it. She's had a copy of the script, of course, but even if she knew it, two days is hardly enough, surely, to use her when she knows nothing of the direction?'

'No, it's not enough,' agreed Max, his voice level and definite. 'And hardly fair to her. Cancel, temporarily for a week, Henry, will you?' He swung round to Leah and addressed her personally for the first time. 'Leah?'

She bestirred herself and said: 'Yes, of course— it means a lot of work for you regarding ticket refunds and publicity, Henry. I'm sorry. I'll be glad to help.'

Henry nodded his acceptance and gazed round at the company. He said generally: 'By the weekend we'll be able to see what sort of shape Nancy will be in.'

'There is a way.'

The words dropped into the brooding silence like a stone into water, the meaning rippling and gaining attention. All eyes turned to the speaker and Charles said:

'What *do* you mean, Oliver?'

Oliver bit his bottom lip and thrust a hand through his dark hair, his eyes going round the group, purposely missing one person in his scrutiny. Frowning, he replied: 'Leah could do it,' and only then did he allow his gaze to rest, almost apologetically, on his producer.

The circle of eyes stayed on him for a split second and then, as one, swept downward to Leah, still sitting on the front row seat. A wave of hot shock swept over her and eyes wide with horrified amazement, she replied abruptly: 'We can do without stupid remarks like that, Oliver.'

As if they were alone, Oliver, undaunted, came forward and sat on the edge of the stage, opposite Leah's seat, his words soft and persuasive. 'You know this play inside out and back to front, Leah, you know you do. You've even rehearsed the part of Elizabeth with Ann, helping her, haven't you? She told me. And you're also an actress, whether you choose to be or not. A damn good actress, Leah. You could do it if you'd let yourself; if we worked hard enough in the time left. If *you're* willing, I'm game.'

The silence was electric. This couldn't be happening to her, thought Leah wildly, not daring to take her eyes from Oliver's face.

'I couldn't do it, Oliver,' she replied warningly, hardening her voice and heart to the faint hint of hope that had immediately sprung up around her.

'Of course she couldn't,' Max said sharply, impatiently. 'How can you suggest such a thing? It's not enough to know the play, Oliver, *you* know that if no one else! There's the sign language to consider.'

Leah caught her breath and Oliver held her gaze, dark and troubled, relentlessly. The seconds ticked away. Leah set her mouth stubbornly and after a long moment allowed the breath to free as a sigh, her lips drooping slightly. The thickly fringed lashes swept down over her eyes, giving him leave, but not helping him.

Oliver waited fractionally and said, slowly and clearly, not taking his eyes from Leah: 'Max, Leah can do sign language. She's fluent.'

Another bombshell. There was a delicate perception among the men present that they were intruding into something private and that Oliver, almost against his will, was being forced to reveal it. The threesome, Max and Leah with Oliver in the middle, seemed isolated and the group round them stood perfectly still, wondering.

As the silence lengthened Leah lifted her lashes and looked at Oliver, then she removed her gaze slowly to Max, who had fixed her with a steady, deliberate regard, eyes coolly speculative in a face that was wiped clean of expression.

Eliot exploded the bomb, totally unaware of any hidden vibrations and in any event only intent on saving his play. He thrust himself into the seat next to Leah, dejection being overtaken by the beginnings of hope.

'Leah! I believe Oliver's right! You *could* do it.' He stared into her face and when she made no reply he turned to the others, expounding his belief. 'Leah learnt sign language when she went deaf—oh, must be over five years ago now. She's been in plays for TFTD. I've worked with her and I know she can do it.'

Oliver lifted his legs and sprang nimbly to his feet on the stage, abruptly, shoulders hunched. This astounding piece of news was being digested and calculated, each face showing something of his thoughts with the exception of one. Max's was like chiselled stone.

Charles was the first to break the silence. He said quietly: 'You gave up acting because you went deaf, Leah?'

She replied a flat: 'Yes.'

'My poor girl,' murmured Charles, and at those words she found her tongue, saying harshly:

'But I can't take Elizabeth. That's just a crazy idea. I haven't acted for five years!'

Oliver turned to her. 'You're still a Union member?' he asked, and after hesitation, Leah nodded, reluctantly. Max swung on his heel and walked downstage, stopping when he came up against the set. The company had all followed his movement but pretended not to. Eliot opened his mouth to speak, but Oliver said sharply: 'Shut up, Eliot,' and the playwright subsided, gave a bewildered glance round, and murmured: 'I don't understand,' while Charles said dryly: 'That's quite obvious, my dear man.'

Leah hardly heard them. She was acutely aware of the tall figure, thinking deeply, downstage. How could everything be so right one minute and so horribly wrong the next? It was like a dream that was rapidly turning into a nightmare.

'I wish you'd all stop looking at me like that,' she said harshly, desperately. 'You're clutching at straws. Don't you think that if I thought there was a chance . . .' and her voice trailed.

'Would you consider giving it a try?' suggested Henry, tentatively, and Oliver added persuasively: 'We could do one scene. See how it goes.'

Max came forward, voice decided, authoritative. 'When is the deadline, Henry? When is the latest we need to make an announcement?'

'I can't do it,' Leah said frantically.

Max glanced down at her, calm and impersonal. 'In that case, we shall cancel. Henry?'

Henry pursed his lips in thought. 'Midday tomorrow, ideally, but we could hang on till four o'clock, give it to the TV networks and radio.' He frowned. 'Yes, I reckon we could get away with four o'clock at a pinch . . . no later.'

'Very well—four it is.'

'Max, I don't want to do it.' The words came out through clenched teeth.

'We all realise that, and sympathise. You can say no at any moment in the time between now and the deadline.'

'You won't let me! If I once say yes to trying, you won't let me!' They could have been alone in the theatre—this was between Max and herself. She said stubbornly: 'What happens if I lose my nerve, just before curtain?'

'If I get you past the deadline, you'll not lose your nerve,' Max told her impassively. 'Leah, have I ever let you down?'

Leah closed her eyes, a mental vision of the now empty theatre packed to capacity. She shot out of her seat and walked rapidly up the aisle and through the double doors, her momentum taking her to the outer exit doors. She burst through them. The bright sunlight was a shock. West 45th Street was a cacophony of sounds, a mixture of traffic, people, pneumatic drills and bulldozers, transistor radios and street vendors. She stood, breathing deeply, taking it all in, the heat a blessed balm to her cold skin. The noise sounded . . . A memory hit her. The noise sounded like music in her ears. Who had she said that to? Ah, yes, to Michael, way back.

Leah turned slowly on her heel. When she was

within a yard of Max she stopped. They seemed not to have movéd. The sounds she had heard out there were still with her, she could still hear them. She said coldly:

'You knew I'd come back,' and then: 'I'll never forgive you for this!'

'I have the feeling you will,' replied Max carefully.

'Does that mean she'll do it?' asked Eliot doubtfully, and Oliver jumped down and took her hands, saying soothingly:

'Good girl! Have a try—that's all you need to do. Charles and I will give you all the help we can.' He hesitated. 'Forgiven me?'

Leah gave a faint smile. Charles said: 'You were right, he did say you'd come back,' and he glanced at Max who had broken away from the group, calling backstage:

'Get the lighting to give us a spot on the area downstage left, will you? Everyone not included in the final scene, make themselves scarce, and I want absolute quiet. Have we a script? Someone give a script to Leah, please.'

'You can always say no,' Charles said quietly, his eyes kind with understanding. 'Max won't allow you to make the wrong decision.'

'Here's the script, Leah.' Eliot thrust the open manuscript into her hands.

'He's starting her with the most difficult scene, isn't he?' murmured Henry, and Charles gave a wry smile.

'As a director, if you can win with a difficult scene, you're more than halfway there.' He turned to Leah. 'Are you ready?' he asked, and silently Leah followed him on stage.

CHAPTER NINE

DURING the next six hours Max worked Leah almost to the point of exhaustion. He gave her no mercy and spared her nothing, until her whole body was consumed with silent hatred for him and life in general.

It was a duel between the two of them, with the rest of the company wary spectators. It was apparent that this was no ordinary director-actress relationship, and those who watched the gradual growth of Leah Durrance in the role of Elizabeth never forgot those agonising, tempestuous hours. So that she was totally submerged in the role, Max had forbidden Leah to speak, not even when they took a break, and the look in those blazing green eyes ensured her isolation.

When Max at last said: 'Okay, we'll call it a day,' more than one person gave a sigh of relief.

Henry took Leah back to the hotel. She was still wound up like a taut spring. When Henry suggested gently that she was allowed to speak now, she ground out:

'Don't encourage me! You might regret it,' and saw Henry smile, but he made no further effort to converse until they reached her hotel bedroom. There he said:

'I've arranged for some sandwiches and a flask of coffee to be put in your room. Try and have something to eat, there's a good girl.' He paused. 'And don't murder him tonight, eh? You'll need him for tomorrow.' He checked the room over and left.

Leah threw the script forcefully down on to the bed, thinking grimly—that bully had better not dare show his face in here!

It was necessary to sustain anger to keep out fear—fear of dying the death on stage and of Max's reaction to the news of her deafness. When the knock came at the door she had showered and donned nightgown and robe and was lying on the bed reading the script. Her eyes lifted and when Max opened the door, she demanded stonily:

'What do you want?'

'I've brought you these, in case they're needed,' Max said calmly, undaunted by her tone. He stepped inside and closed the door behind him.

'What are they?' Leah asked ungraciously, then: 'If they're sleeping pills, you can take them away. I don't want them.' She watched him place the bottle on the bedside table and went on truculently: 'I shall probably have nightmares all night!' She glared at him and he stared back, silent. The last six hours didn't seem to have affected him much, she thought resentfully. He had showered and changed his working jeans and sweat-shirt for summer-weight trousers and a pale blue open-necked shirt. She dropped her eyes from him to the script, saying: 'Now that you've done your errand of mercy . . .' Her voice trailed pointedly, but she was not surprised when the script was whipped from her hands and placed out of reach on the dressing-table.

'I told you not to look at that again tonight. Give it a rest.'

'That's easier said than done, with tomorrow night looming up on the horizon!'

'I fail to see why you're so mad at me,' Max said reasonably. 'If you'd refused to have had a go you'd never have forgiven yourself. You can still say no. No one can force you to go on stage if you really don't want to, now can they?' He paused and tilted her a look. 'Will it make you sleep any easier if I say that you'll be all right, Leah?'

She curled her lip. 'You acting God today, Max?'

'That seems to be the role you're insisting I'm playing. I'm merely going on what I've seen during the past six hours and what I know of your capabilities in the past.' He moved a couple of paces nearer the bed and looked down at her speculatively. 'I'll even go so far as to challenge your defensive attitude. Of course you're worried about tomorrow ...'

'You're damn right I am!' she flared, swinging herself indignantly from the bed, her eyes sparkling angrily. 'I wasn't lying when I said I'd lost my nerve, and at this particular moment I'm scared sick!'

Max held up a hand to stop the torrent. 'I believe you. But I also know that by the time we finished tonight something was taking over that fear. The adrenalin was beginning to flow again, and whether you admit it or not, by the end you were only interested in Elizabeth's feelings and not Leah's.' He didn't wait for an answer and glanced down at the sandwiches, covered in protective film-wrap, which were untouched. 'Aren't you going to eat anything?'

'I've told you, I feel sick. And how can you talk about past capabilities? That was five years ago!'

'"Talent is faith in oneself, one's own powers",' Max quoted, and leah mocked:

'That's very easy to say, but it's me that'll be in the firing line!'

'Exactly! My faith in you isn't enough. You'll decide tomorrow at four whether your own faith will take you there.'

Leah, about to reply, was interrupted by a knock, a discreet tap, at the door, and Max went to open it, returning with a tray on which stood a bottle and two glasses.

Leah raised her brows. 'May one ask what this is for?'

'An alternative to sleeping pills,' he replied, pulling the cork and pouring wine into the two glasses. He handed her one of them. 'Here's to first nights,' and he toasted her, eyes dark above the rim.

'Here's to Nancy's miraculous recovery,' retorted Leah, and took a sip. It was cold and delicious. Sarcastically, she asked: 'Is this a replay of the seduction scene?' In the game of chess, when your pieces are weak on defence, attack with your strongest weapon.

'That's what I'd planned,' admitted Max easily; whatever his real feelings, they were being remarkably hidden. 'Either that or the quarrel scene.'

'I have a choice?'

After a long scrutiny, he said: 'So be it. The quarrel scene it is. Shall I begin? I think you'll agree I have grounds.' He paused. 'Who knew you were going deaf?'

Leah drained her glass and held it out for a refill. 'My doctor and Una Bell.' She held his stare, goading him.

'You didn't think I'd be interested in knowing what was happening to you?'

She gave a disdainful shrug of the shoulders, the silk sheen of the robe catching the light. 'I didn't consider it to be any of your business.'

Max's mouth tightened, and a nerve throbbed in his jaw. 'You mean to hurt, don't you? You really want your row, don't you, Leah?' He poured the wine into her glass, his face suddenly austere.

He was containing himself with an effort, Leah judged, and wondered what she had to say that would make him lose control. It was an interesting speculation. Perhaps she'd find out ... she took another drink, saying:

'This wine isn't a bad idea. If I get drunk, the bogies might leave me alone.'

'They might, but I won't.' Max pulled her round to face him and some of the wine splashed down the front of the robe. 'So—you don't think it was any of my business! Good God, woman! what did you take me for?'

'A man who wanted no commitments. Simple as that.'

'Nothing's as simple as that. You're fooling yourself. By living together we both held a degree of commitment.'

'Really? Does that mean you're committed to Stephanie Farrel? She'll be awfully glad to hear it!'

The dark eyes became hooded and with restraint, ice in his voice, Max asked: 'What the hell does that mean, I wonder?' and as comprehension widened his eyes, he went on, dangerously quiet: 'Thank you. Now we know where we stand. I'm not going to deny that my relationship with Stephanie hasn't been platonic, or that during the past five years there haven't been any other women in my life—those years are none of your damned business. What I deeply resent is the suggestion that I'm capable of making love to you on a whim—do you really believe that? There has never been a committed relationship between myself and Stephanie Farrel. She borrowed my apartment while I was in the States last year and moved into her own house on my return. You're the only woman I've ever asked to share my roof.'

A faint pink tinged Leah's cheeks. 'I considered my deafness concerned only myself. Either of us could break our relationship. If you'd wanted, eventually, to finish, it would have been rather difficult for you to have kicked me out, deaf and with a broken career at my feet, wouldn't it?' She gave a twisted smile. 'I saved you the decision.'

'Thank you again,' Max snapped grimly. 'I prefer making my own.'

'Very well, I'll re-phrase that. I saved myself the humiliation of a relationship existing on pity!' With a smothered oath, Max swung away and stood for a moment, his back turned to her. She went on inexorably: 'I could have ended up totally deaf. How does that strike you? Remember your views on the happy ending to the play? Rather significant, don't you think?'

He swung back to her. 'Rubbish! I was basing my opinion on the characters portrayed. By no stretch of the imagination are we anything like them. You . . .' He broke off, his anger mounting. 'Why should you suppose I would eventually kick you out?'

Leah took a drink, lifting a disdainful shoulder. 'Affairs do finish usually, don't they? Especially if there's someone ready and willing to step into the vacant side of the bed.'

'I shall *never* believe that Alison Brett was anything to do with your decision to go.' His voice was a cold whiplash. 'Be very careful, Leah, you're beginning to make me exceedingly angry. But that's what you want, isn't it? You're getting back at me for a number of reasons, and may I deserve it and my shoulders are broad enough.' The dark eyes glinted warningly. He inclined his head with exaggerated courtesy. 'You were, I believe, referring to Alison Brett.'

'I was. And I'm sorry to disappoint you, but in my dark moments I did wonder if she was to be my replacement.'

'Then you were a fool.'

'Possibly. I wasn't at my most coherent during that period.' Green eyes were locked with blazing brown.

'Alison Brett,' said Max plainly, 'is a pain in the neck, but a good actress. Sometimes I'm forced to work with good actresses who think they're God's gift and who are thick-skinned and totally one-track-minded.' He paused, jaw clenched. 'I was under the impression that we understood each other enough for you to know that. How dare you consider . . .' He broke off, the pallor in his face very apparent.

The wine was beginning to work, the tension within her was easing, and it was extremely satisfying to watch the expert in restraint and control finally losing his temper.

'I beg your pardon. I'll apologise if it will make you feel any better.' Leah flapped a hand airily. 'She was used as an excuse, how's that?'

There was a silence following on this statement that she did not understand.

'You *needed* an excuse?'

The glass was arrested at her lips and her lashes shot up as she eyed him warily. What had she said to make him pounce like that? Excuse? The blush swept upwards from her throat. She crashed the glass down on to the tray and said abruptly:

'If you want me to act tomorrow you'd better go. I must get some sleep.'

'You needed an excuse?' demanded Max, the inquisitor, a glitter of triumph in his eyes.

She swung round and shouted: 'Yes, damn you! I needed an excuse! I didn't want to go! Is that what you want me to say?'

He grasped her by the upper arms and pulled her to him.

'Yes!—and more. Would it help if I told you that when I found you gone I was like a man kicked in the gut? That I couldn't stay in the same room as you that first time we met again at Celia's, because seeing you laughing and talking made me realise that I hadn't got over you and that realisation brought on a violence of feeling against myself and you that I had to get out? Why do you suppose I should feel like that if I didn't love you, need you to distraction?' He shook her, saying harshly: 'If you ever walk out on me again—*for any reason*—I'll ... I'll ...' and then his mouth was on hers, ruthlessly demanding, and Leah, in return, wildly giving. They parted, breathing heavily, eyes locked, and with a choking sob she buried her head against his chest, crying:

'Oh, Max, I do love you so,' and heard his grim: 'So I should think!' and her fingers closed into his hair and he was holding her high against his chest, letting her slide slowly downwards against him, their lips meeting again, gently, tenderly, at first, and then with consuming urgency. The robe fell to the floor, followed by the nightgown, lying in a shimmer of cream silk at her feet. An arm circled her waist, strong and masterful, and Max was lifting her up and cradling her to him. With his lips close to hers, he murmured quizzically:

'What follows the quarrel scene, madam producer?'

Unerringly twisting each tiny button through its hole until the palms of her hands could smooth the shirt away and over his broad shoulders, Leah replied huskily: 'I never tell my director how to do his job,' and then there was no need for words, only sensation after sensation and a tumultuous storm of feeling that finally burst into a million fragments of exquisite sweetness and brilliance that settled into two heartbeats, beating as one.

Max smoothed a frond of hair from Leah's cheek and groaned:

'What a fearful amount of time we've wasted. Five bloody years!'

She shifted more comfortably into the valley between his arm and body. 'You weren't missing me every single minute,' she teased, and he gave a short laugh.

'You'd be surprised how often you loomed into my mind. The worst, I admit, was at the beginning, followed by a period of barren waste in the middle when I decided finally and irrevocably never again to allow any woman to have the power to make me go through that trauma. Then at Celia's I realised I wasn't free of you. When I called the following day, having gained some measure of control, and Celia told me you'd returned to London, I even felt relief. I could learn to forget you all over again.' He gave another laugh, self-mocking, and Leah twisted round, easing her form to his. Max touched her cheek. 'If we'd talked then, would you have told me why you'd left me, do you think?'

Leah brushed her lips across his chest, salty with perspiration, and looked up into his eyes. 'If you'd asked me to fly with you to the moon, I'd have said yes,' she replied simply.

'Ah, well!' His hand absently trailed her back. 'Despite all my good intentions, I couldn't resist keeping track of you through Henry via Michael—very discreetly, you understand—and when Michael rang me to say he had a play he thought I'd be interested in, and that the producer was to be a certain Leah Durrance, I came over.' He paused and went on thoughtfully: 'My feelings were extremely mixed at that point. The play sounded good. I considered Michael to have a keen judgment and when I read it I wasn't disappointed. That you were to be producer was something else entirely—a bonus, if you like. I came, I told myself, out of curiosity, and not out of need. The minute I saw you I got the punch in the gut again and knew I was nowhere over you.'

'Which is why you were so angry,' soothed Leah, and Max grinned.

'Which is why I was so angry ... and the curiosity was still there. You see, I couldn't accept that explanation of yours, and I did think that you'd probably left me for someone else, and then you denied that, and I was inclined to believe you. Gradually, I came to realise that you were not so indifferent to my charms as you'd like me to believe.'

'And how!' breathed Leah, laughing softly.

'There was this guy, too, hovering around, who was providing a good smoke-screen.'

'Poor Eliot!'

'Poor Eliot, my eye!' mocked her love. 'The poor slob wouldn't have known what had hit him. He'll be much better off with Ann, and if I read the signs right, seeing her lying in that hospital bed today has probably brought the guy to his senses. As for Oliver, did he know, I wonder, how near he was to violence today? God in heaven! I deeply resented him knowing *anything* about you that I didn't know!'

'He was aware of that fact,' said Leah dryly. 'I very nearly hit him myself.' She raised herself up on to one elbow and asked: 'Does Henry know about us too, do you think?'

'Mmm?' Max brushed his lips across the tip of a breast that was invitingly near, and for some moments Leah lost her train of thought. With an effort she remembered, and murmured: 'Henry. Do you think he knows?'

'I guess both Henry and Michael fitted the jigsaw pieces together pretty soon, between them. Henry knew I was in deep with someone over in England around the time Joss died, and you'd told Michael part of our story, and I imagine they soon put their heads together. Celia only realised you were important when I suggested she ask you to stay. I've never done that before. It was all she needed to hear wedding bells!' His lips curved. 'Is Celia going to hear them, Leah?'

Her heart turned a funny somersault at the look in his eyes. 'Mr Calvert! Is this a proposal of marriage?' she asked primly, and as his hands tightened warningly, she added: 'Yes, yes, oh yes, please!'

After a satisfying moment Max lifted his head and held her slightly away, saying: 'You realise you'll hate me all over again tomorrow, don't you?'

Leah gave a gurgle of laughter deep in her throat, and murmured: 'I've always known you could be a devil to work for.' Her eyes flew open,

wide with sudden consternation. 'Max! I've just
remembered tomorrow!' and there was anguish in
her voice.

'Then I shall have to make you forget, shan't I?'
said Max.

How many of those out there, clapping and
shouting 'Bravo!' will go home thinking of a
happy ending? Leah wondered, as she took her
bow, Charles holding one hand, Oliver the other.
How many times had they bowed, for goodness'
sake? Max was there, standing in the wings. She
turned her head and smiled a radiant smile for him
alone. How drained he looked! she thought in
surprise, and then—good heavens, he's gone
through agony for me tonight. Another bow. She
smiled first at Oliver, who grinned delightedly, and
then at Charles, who raised her hand to his lips.
The audience liked that. She glanced at Max again
and found he was smiling. It was difficult to
believe that all this was happening. That she was
going to marry Max; that she had conquered her
fears and was acting again. She remembered the
heady perfume of the flowers that filled her
dressing room and the numerous telegrams of
good wishes; the excitement and anticipation as
the theatre filled; the underlying rumble of nerves
dispelled after the first few electrifying minutes of
the play.

She stepped back, releasing hands, and Oliver
and Charles were on their own, surprised,
acknowledging her public gesture of thanks for
their tremendous support. They took their bows.
Leah found that her cheeks were wet. How silly to
cry when she was so happy! Now the two men
were leading her forward and she was on her own

and the volume of applause increased and there was the sound of feet stamping. A bouquet was being handed up. Would the curtain come down now? Surely! But no—the call came for 'Author!' and Eliot joined them, diffidently, and finally the curtain came down slowly and it was all over.

There was a round of applause from the other diners as Leah walked into Sardi's, flanked by Charles and Oliver. She was wearing her favourite colour, emerald green, the top and trousers very similar in style and texture to that other outfit she had been wearing the first evening with Max, after *Arms and the Man*. As then, the jewelled spider was at her throat, and as then, a small box had been delivered to the dressing-room prior to the performance. That piece of jewellery was adorning the third finger of her left hand.

Michael, who with Ruth had flown over for the first night on Broadway, came to meet her, smiling broadly, kissing her hand and leading her, like Royalty, to their table, saying:

'Leah, my lovely, you are incomparable!' and Ruth hugged her hard, whispering, 'You were wonderful, Leah, just wonderful! I cried my eyes out!'

'Have you sent the bouquet to Nancy at the hospital?' Leah asked anxiously, and Michael said:

'Don't worry, it's all been seen to, and she's doing fine. Sends her love.' He grinned. 'We have a surprise for you, Leah. Look who's here!' and drew back and Una beamed at her from the other side of the table.

Nearly crying, Leah flung herself at her friend, and as they embraced, Una said gruffly:

'Always knew that's where you should be, treading the boards, and I might have guessed that he'd be the one to make you do it,' and Una turned her head and looked up at Max, standing watching them gravely. He smiled, his eyes amused, remembering, and catching Una's eye Leah blushed and then laughed, also remembering, and murmured:

'You were right about something else too, Una,' and Una frowned, looked from Max to Leah and grinned, saying: 'About time!'

A glass was put into Leah's hand and delicious Sardi specialities were brought to the table and, surprised, she found that she was hungry. In between eating and talking she allowed her gaze to wander over the hundreds of caricatures of famous theatrical stars, past and present, lining the restaurant's walls. Would hers ever be here? she wondered quixotically. In her mind's eye she could see a line sketch, the hair drawn back in a ponytail as she had worn it for most of the play, large cat's eyes—perhaps a pair of hands in the foreground caught in the act of signing a word. She grinned at the outrageous thought and caught Max's eyes. He signed: 'I love you,' and her smile deepened and she signed back: 'I love you. I even love spiders!' and he threw back his head and laughed.

Ruth, catching sight of the sparkle as Leah's hands moved in sign language, exclaimed in awful tones: 'Leah! You're wearing a ring!'

Talking was suspended and everyone stared at the emerald ring on her finger.

'About time,' said Michael with satisfaction, innocently repeating Una's words, and grasping Max warmly by the hand. 'Congratulations, Max. Full marks for perseverance.'

'Michael Walsh,' said Ruth in an awesome

voice, 'do you mean to tell me that you've been holding out on this very important information?'

'Couldn't tell you what I didn't know,' defended Michael, 'and you should be commiserating with me, because I suspect I'm about to lose a damn good producer.'

Celia brushed her lips against Leah's cheek and whispered: 'Oh, I am so glad. Be happy!' and Henry smiled, and said: 'Welcome, sister-in-law,' and to Max: 'Congratulations, feller—second time lucky!'

Leah met Eliot's eyes across the table and gave him a tentative smile. He looked pointedly at Max, eyebrows raised, and when she gave a small nod, he mouthed: 'Good luck,' while Ann, a little pale, her arm in a plaster and sling, sitting by his side, beamed happily at the news.

Charles rose to give a toast after bottles of champagne had mysteriously appeared, and their names were enthusiastically coupled, and Max, joining her, gave her a brief kiss, amidst cheers and clapping.

Oliver yawned and stated: 'At least it's taken our minds off the papers,' while Henry groaned: 'Oh, God! the papers!'

'I forgot to order them!' exclaimed Leah, stricken, and Max smiled at her distress and soothed: 'I remembered. They're being delivered here.'

'Are we staying until they come out?' asked Ann delightedly, and Oliver replied: 'Could you sleep? We might as well wait here, drinking champagne.'

After a while, when the exuberance had settled down into friends talking quietly together, Max turned to Leah and murmured:

'Coming for a ride?'

He was wearing the white tuxedo and to Leah's eyes looked extremely distinguished. 'To the moon?' she queried with a teasing smile, and rose to her feet. They drifted away, their going noticed but not remarked.

Max lifted a hand to a prowling taxi, saying: 'Just drive around, will you?' and the cabby gave a laconic: 'Sure,' and yawned, thinking yearningly of his bed, shooting the glass dividing partition into place.

Max settled Leah in his arms. He kissed her upturned face. 'Tired?' he asked.

She replied dreamily: 'I don't know. I don't seem to know anything.'

'Oh, yes, you do.'

She swept him a glance and lifted her hand to admire the ring. 'Ah, now that I can hardly believe.'

'You will,' promised Max.

The cab cruised down Broadway, turned into 42nd Street and swung left into the Avenue of the Americas.

'Max, what did Henry mean?'

'I've no idea,' remarked Max comfortably.

'When he said second time lucky?' Leah felt him still and she sat up so that she could see his face more clearly. She went on quietly: 'He meant that you were going to ask me to marry you before, didn't he?'

Max shrugged and took her hand, touching his lips to her fingers. 'When Joss died, I was suddenly made aware of my own mortality. We talked late one night, Henry and I ... about families and what we wanted from life, and I intimated that there was a girl I wanted to marry—if she'd have me. I remember Henry asked me if she would have me and I said I didn't know. I said that she was a girl with a strong commitment to her career and that I'd made it rather clear at the outset that marriage wasn't on the agenda. However, I was going to get back as quickly as I could and ask her.'

'Oh, Max!' mourned Leah, going into his arms. 'And I wasn't there!'

'My own fault. I was a fool not to have asked you before. It brought me down a peg or two and probably did me good,' he drawled. 'And I wasn't able to help you, comfort you when you needed it, was I? Because of my damned non-commitment.' He smiled down at her. 'We're not the same people now, are we? We might stand a better chance of knowing what we nearly missed.' He glanced out of the window. 'He's taking us past 45th Street— here's the theatre.'

Traffic lights at the junction halted them almost outside the theatre. They could see the billboards, bold in their announcement that *The Chequered Silence* was being presented now, at this theatre. The lights changed and they moved on. Max, looking at his watch, tapped the glass, signalling that they wanted to return to Sardi's, and the cabby nodded.

The sky was getting lighter. Leah wondered at the traffic on the roads and people still around, then laughed to herself—in the Big Apple there was absolutely no need to go to bed if you didn't want to, there was always something to do, somewhere to go.

They walked into Sardi's, Max's arm round Leah's shoulder, and stopped as one, looking across the restaurant to their table. Papers were spread out over the surface of the table and everyone was being hugged and kissed, jumping up and down, cheering and laughing, and Henry was waving a champagne bottle in the air and waiters were refilling glasses and the whole room was in an uproar.

Max smiled down at Leah, his arm tightening. 'It looks to me, my love, that we have a hit on our hands.'

Leah smiled up at him happily. 'So it does,' she replied. and they began to walk towards the table, then they were seen and the table erupted and they all surged to meet them.